MURDER AT
PROSPECT KENTUCKY

MURDER AT
PROSPECT KENTUCKY

AUGUSTA WALLACE LYONS

G. P. PUTNAM'S SONS · NEW YORK

SBN: 399-12067-x

Library of Congress Cataloging in Publication Data

Lyons, Augusta Wallace,
    Murder at Prospect, Kentucky.

    I. Title.
PZ4.L9899Mu   [PS3562.Y447]   813'.5'4   77-24462

MURDER AT
PROSPECT KENTUCKY

Prologue

HETTIE KELLER MADE Miz Purdie drop her off in front of the Prospect Store. "I want to walk home from here," she insisted. "I been reading them articles as how walking's good for your heart. It's three miles from the store to home, and I walks three miles every evening."

She didn't do any such fool thing, of course. Not after walking the floors of the Springdale Nursing Home eight hours a day, five days a week, with a mop and a scrub bucket. But the good Lord in His mercy forgives white lies, she hoped.

And she didn't want nobody to know how far she really would walk—just the short piece along Highway 42, uphill from the store, to the Ashton place. She'd look stupid if her reasons for going there turned out to be wrong. If she was right—and she'd bet her life she was—the less said to anybody the better. Anybody except Mr. Ashton, that is.

She stood in front of the store, lit up and still open, until Miz Purdie's car started towards Louisville, then walked in the opposite direction, slowly along the highway, keeping close to the ditch. The way some folks drove these days, pedestrians had to look out for theirselves. Real careful, too.

She left the highway at the second driveway on the left: Paul Ashton's, a curving road bordered with ancient hedges. There weren't no better lawyer nowhere than Paul Ashton, and him being Miz Morgan's nephew wouldn't hurt none neither.

No better lawyer and no living soul with a worse kept driveway. The blacktop all tore up into potholes you could break an ankle in at noontime of a warm, sunny day. Let alone now with the snow and the failing light making it look smooth as a hospital bed sheet.

She picked her way carefully, determined but not in a hurry. She needed a few minutes to figure out how to tell Mr. Ashton what she knew. Naturally Ginelda—it was Ginelda, the Morgans' cook, she'd dropped by to have a visit with on her way back from the nursing home—thought that terrible scream they all heard came out of a nightmare. Like Miz Morgan's nurses—Purdie and them—said. Natural for them nurses to think that, too. Being used to only private cases with lots of family around, paying doctors to do everything they can to make the sick one comfortable—they didn't hear much screaming. Not like she did at Springdale.

After eight years at Springdale, she knew about all kinds of screaming. Nightmare screams always come out scrambled. Not more'n one or two words clear, if they was any clear at all. With senile screaming, or delirium, the words was clear often as not. And even sometimes strung together so as to

10

make sense. But not deep, thought-out kind of sense, like she heard from Miz Morgan. Not the same tone of sense.

That poor little old woman believed somebody wanted to kill her. Probably for her money. And Hettie Keller took her serious, on account of that tone of sense, or knowing, in her screaming, no matter who else didn't. Ginelda, the nurses, they didn't none of them have her experience. She wished she hadn't had it either. But maybe it was meant to be, so's she could save Miz Morgan. Anyways, the folks at Springdale would be even worse off if the floors wasn't scrubbed.

Stepping carefully, she rounded a box-hedged curve, and saw the Ashton house. She stopped in her tracks, feeling her heart was about to pop right out her chest. The house lay long, low and white in the almost dark. With not a light in it, and no cars in the carport. Nobody home. Just her alone at the edge of night, having on her mind the frighteningest thoughts.

The Ashtons could be anywheres. At one of their fancy clubs, out to dinner. Maybe wouldn't come home until midnight. Or later.

The silence, the loneliness, and the cold scared her. So did the weight of what she wanted to tell, with maybe no way now to tell it in time to do any good. Then a glow of light penetrated the curve of the boxwood behind her, like a blessing from heaven, and headlights rounded the curve, bathing her in their glare. She turned toward them with such joyful relief that her arms spread wide as if to embrace the welcome car.

But something went wrong. The car lurched forward with sudden speed, toward her. Like it was aiming at her.

"Skidding," she thought as she leapt out of the way,

11

nimbly but not quite nimbly enough. One fender caught her at the hip, spun her around, and she fell flat on her face across the middle of the road.

The car went into reverse.

"Nothing's broke," she said aloud, as she started to scramble to her feet, eager to assure Mr. Ashton that the accident hadn't really hurt her, and that she wasn't one to sue on account of a bruise.

Just as she got up onto her hands and knees, the car charged at her again. The left wheels went over her legs. The right wheels crushed her chest.

Her brain life lasted just enough to form the astonished thought: "Killed . . . on purpose."

The car backed up again.

Hettie Keller's head, not visibly damaged, lay with one cheek cushioned in the snow. The other side of her pale face—its wrinkles forming patterns that suggested kindness, dignity, and amazement—still looked alive. A lock of gray hair, threaded with brown, moved in the wind.

The driver of the car veered a bit to the right and drove slowly forward over the aging face. Then backed over it again. Not for pleasure. Just for insurance against further movement.

CHAPTER I

THE TWO DOORS of Harry Morgan's aged, cream-colored convertible were decorated with large-lettered, blood-red signs, scrawled in his own erratic but legible hand: "This car is unlocked. Persons who wish to enter it for theft or other purposes are respectfully requested to use the doors, rather than slash their way through the canvas top."

He parked beside another sign. It was attached to a wooden stile in the high, barbed wire fence that separated the sunny pastures of his own cattle farm from his father's wilderness. The message, neat black on white, read: "No hunting or fishing allowed. Trespassers will be prosecuted to the full extent of the law."

And Harry had always known that this meant being cooked in the electric chair, if his father, Tom, could have his way. Somebody really would be cooked soon, if Hettie

Keller's killer came before a local jury. But it wasn't likely he ever would.

Martha Sneedon and a customer were the last persons known to have seen Hettie alive. Prospect residents called Martha, who owned the Prospect Store, "the best seeing-eye human in three counties." Just before closing the store last night, she had helped a local customer carry out some packages and saw Hettie's back as she plodded up the highway.

"I wonder where Hettie Keller's going," Martha had remarked to the customer. "She lives in the other direction, on Covered Bridge Road, same as you."

Martha had told the police she had watched the customer drive off and turn into Covered Bridge Road. His wife, two grown sons, and a hired man saw him drive into his own garage about five minutes later.

Of course, that only proved the customer didn't do it. Even seeing-eye Martha missed some things—like whose car, or even what kind of car, turned into the Ashton driveway and came out again around 5 P.M., while Martha was still tending the store.

The Ashtons themselves easily proved Betty Lou met Paul up at his office in Louisville a few minutes before five and that he and she went directly from there to the Pendennis Club for drinks and a dinner party.

A heavy snowfall, lasting from 5:30 to 10 P.M. had obliterated earlier tire tracks and covered Hettie's body. Only the unexpected white mound, strangely grave-shaped, made Paul Ashton stop his car a few yards short of his carport and investigate it, without running over it.

Harry himself, and his poor little wife, Katinka, were each

14

other's alibis. Katinka knew Harry had been in the barn and Harry knew Katinka was in the house with their children. Katinka, icily composed while the police questioned her gently, went to bed when they left, cowering under too many covers like a terrified child. She didn't understand that since Hettie had last been seen alive after leaving Tom Morgan's home and going to the Ashtons, the police would routinely seek information from her and anyone else connected with her husband's family, or the Ashtons, without seriously suspecting any of them. They unquestioningly accepted Harry's statement that at approximately the time of the murder, he'd been in the barn with fourteen cows, and Katinka's that she'd been with her children. Alone. The oldest child, Sarah, six, hadn't gotten home from a birthday party. That left Naomi, two, and Rachel, nine months, to confirm her story.

As Harry stood beside his convertible, he reviewed the facts: It was now widespread knowledge that Hettie had left the Springdale Nursing Home at 3 P.M. When the nurse who took her home around 4:30 was closely interrogated, she swore Hettie had discussed only the threatening snowstorm and conditions at Springdale and then had insisted on being dropped in front of the store. Evidently she had gone from there to the Ashtons. Why?

The nurses and Ginelda couldn't hazard a guess. Neither could anybody at Springdale. She hadn't made any phone calls from the Morgans or, as far as anyone knew, from Springdale. As far as could be determined, she'd never in her life phoned the Ashtons, or been to their house, or to Paul Ashton's office.

So whom could the police suspect? Harry could see no

way by which the murder of Hettie Keller would ever be solved. One of those perfect crimes that, as they say, don't happen.

Harry left the car, climbed over the stile to check on his father's property, property he would very soon inherit, and strode down the steep, heavily wooded hillside in a zigzag line, searching right and left in the sleet-covered snow for human footprints. Not that he expected to find any.

Everyone in Jefferson and Oldham counties knew that for over half a century his father had taken long tramps through his woods twice every day: before an early breakfast, and at about this time, after his day's work at the newspaper, to look for any traces of intruders, especially poachers.

They also knew, of course, that he'd been flattened by a stroke six weeks ago, but as long as the old man kept on breathing, there was precious little chance of his territory being invaded. Even when he was six feet under, his Bible Belt neighbors, some of whom saw ghosts now and then, would be likely to avoid the slightest risk of meeting him here.

In 1889, Harry's father was seized by the conviction—he never had opinions, only convictions—that the nation's greatest need was more wilderness, great expanses of it throughout the country and small patches dotted about at frequent intervals near cities. By 1911 he'd saved enough to buy the makings of his own dot, a farm twelve miles from Louisville. This part of it, from the top of the hill to the lonely loop of the creek below that formed its farthest boundary, had been virgin forest even then. The rest had been cultivated, but when Tom Morgan took possession, he allowed all of it, except the yard around the house, the adjacent cabin, and the grape arbor, to revert to its pre-Daniel Boone condition. He kept even the snakes and poison ivy safe from death at human hands.

Wherever the underbrush beneath the towering, leafless trees grew thick enough to conceal anything, Harry, like a dutiful game warden, pushed it aside with his walking stick, on the off chance that a steel trap might be hidden there.

The gnarled stick looked like a natural extension of Harry. Years of heavy labor in the fields, alongside his tenants, had hardened his body oak-strong, and weathered his skin to match the color of the dark wood, though not the gleam. Much handling had smoothed the well-aged stick to a shine, even a primitive kind of style, otherwise entirely lacking in Harry's appearance.

His Navy winter overcoat had been liberated from spit and polish since the last time he wore it in the line of duty, over twenty years ago, on the Murmansk route. The cap had somehow got lost, so his head was uncovered. Totally uncovered. He'd turned bald at the age of twenty-four, except for a narrow line of wiry brown hair that grew around the back of his head from the top of one ear to the top of the other, making it look like a brown egg with a matching fur collar.

Near the foot of the hill, fifty yards above the creek, there was a huge outcropping of rock with trees towering above it. His sister, Essie, had called it "Fairy Castle" nearly forty years ago, and the name had stuck. The trees that covered the top of it now were tall and thick-trunked, but Harry remembered their sapling days. Tom had often brought him and Essie here to play on a Sunday afternoon so Estelle could get a rest, and invariably he tried to make good use of the enforced association by explaining the importance of reforestation.

Harry had now seen enough. He could assure Tom this afternoon, as he had every afternoon since the stroke, that his land still looked as it must have on the sixth day, when God said, "Let the earth bring forth the living creatures after his kind," and created Adam and Eve, *without*, Tom always maintained, giving them any such absurd order as to "be fruitful and multiply."

Harry agreed it was illogical to believe the Creator didn't know as much as Malthus. So obviously some poor monk started over-population by mistranslating holy writ from one dead language to another. As a small boy, Harry had been subjected to some jocular teasing from fathers of his friends—men *their* sons called "Dad"—about Tom's over-population hang-up. They said Tom started doing lead editorials on the subject the morning after Harry's birth.

Before the birth of his first child, Essie, Tom decreed that all his descendants should call him and his wife by their first names, Tom and Estelle. It had bothered Harry not to have a "mom" and "dad" like everyone else, especially a "dad." Until the moment he decided to learn to do without one.

On a soft spring evening, at the age of fifteen, he had come to the dinner table with a black eye and an inner certainty that he would never know happiness again. He had fallen in love several weeks earlier with a girl named Mary Jane Cropper. Other men could have Helen of Troy, the Blessed Damozel, and all the movie stars in Hollywood. He wanted only Mary Jane. Not to have seen her was not to have *lived*. He felt a benign pity for all males doomed to go

18

through life without enjoying this earthly form of the beatific vision. Then one afternoon, another guy, a senior—Harry was only a sophomore—asked her to a dance she'd promised to attend with him and she accepted. A confrontation with his rival resulted in nothing more than the shiner.

All he remembered now of that devastating heartbreak was getting so carried away by grief and outrage that he referred to his successful rival as "that goddam bastard," at table, in the hearing of his entire family.

Tom, who never punished his children, not once in their lives, raised his voice like Jehovah at his worst, and roared, "I will not tolerate such language in the presence of ladies! Miss Cropper displayed excellent judgment in spurning you for a more gentlemanly admirer."

Harry gripped his steak knife, wondering if he was strong enough to kill Tom. He wasn't. Not at that age. So instead, he made an instant resolution to use as few words as possible of any kind to Tom, until he could feel sure he was safe from ever again trying to tell him anything that mattered.

This had taken an entire year, during which he didn't speak to Tom (or to Estelle or Essie in Tom's presence) except to answer direct questions as briefly as courtesy permitted. Usually he could make do with "yes" or "no" pronounced in a tone of impeccable but cold politeness.

Tom's reaction was: "If the confounded youngster wants to play monosyllabic idiot, let him! I've spent years on end 'guessing' the riddles and laughing at the 'jokes' Cain and Abel bored Adam with. And *this* at an age when I'm frequently told my brain cells have been dying for decades already. Dying at the rate of twenty-five thousand cells a day, according to what Harry used to announce gleefully several times a week, before he stopped communicating. Or is it twenty-five million? The cells in which I deposited the exact figure seem to have joined the dear departed."

Essie often said, "The one thing Tom couldn't do, even to please Estelle, was just to enjoy a child of any age. He never even wanted to hold a small one on his lap occasionally. Or a large one either."

Harry broke into a malicious smile recalling two small creatures that did manage to spend a great deal of time on Tom's lap, blissfully impervious to signals of rejection that no other infant—furred, feathered, or human—had failed to detect.

When Harry was ten, the owner of a farm contiguous to the Morgan wilderness shot a pair of crows during the nesting season. Rather than let their half-grown fledglings starve to death, Tom climbed up to their high nest and, handling them with considerable distaste, brought them home to Essie to raise. They thrived and Essie loved them, but Tom, they were irrevocably convinced, was their mother. Every evening when he came home from his office, they greeted him with loud caws of ecstasy. When he sat out in the yard to enjoy the flowers which spilled across the lawn between his ancient maples and birches, the crows would hop onto his lap, competing with fierce sibling rivalry for the best spot, the place closest to his shirt front, against which the winner yearningly pressed its nearly featherless body from which, to Estelle's consternation, things other than flowers often spilled.

Tom couldn't quite bring himself to hurt their feelings by actually pushing them off, so he sat—rigid, miserable, enduring—with both of them on his knees, consoling himself with the thought that birds grow up fast and that therefore the two crows would soon get over their infernal, infantile taste for cuddling.

But they didn't—neither their taste nor their natural functions. When they acquired adult plumage and learned to fly, they no longer had to wait for him to sit down to demonstrate their devotion. Whenever he stepped out of the house, they swooped down from the roof to land on his shoulders and rub their heads tenderly against his cheeks.

Tom began to place his hopes for deliverance in the call of the wild that would come the following spring with the mating season, but it didn't. Flocks of wild crows flew over the house with inviting caws, but the Morgan crows always cawed back on a note of unmistakable anger. It was not until their third spring that they rejoined their own kind, returning only occasionally to visit Tom. He lived in dread that they would eventually bring their progeny to call, or even leave them on his doorstep, but they didn't.

A suitable epitaph for Tom, Harry thought, would be: "Here lies a man deeply loved by one woman and two crows."

For the present, Tom lay helpless in a hospital bed installed on the sun porch off the kitchen, ostensibly only a breath away from the time when that epitaph, or another, would be inscribed. Estelle had ordered him placed there when he was brought home a week ago from the Norton Infirmary.

"Why? Why not in the back bedroom upstairs?" Harry had asked her. "Where you could walk in, speak to him, now and then."

"No!" she had answered. "The further away from me he is, the less likely they ... "

These mysterious "theys" had only recently come up, and the references worried Harry. Was Estelle getting potty? It was only since his father's fall that she had not been feeling well—maybe she was afraid Tom might catch whatever ailed her. But that still didn't explain the "theys." "They, Estelle? They ... who?"

But she refused to answer. She just looked at him out of deep-sunk eyes that seemed to see something he didn't and said, "Don't argue, Harry. Put him on the sun porch. He'll like being down there close to his trees."

Because of her behavior, her temporary physical weakness and high blood pressure, the doctor convinced her and Harry that she should be confined to bed except for occasional walks around the room or down the hall and necessary trips to the bathroom. The doctor explained all this to Harry and Harry's niece, Star, who had come west from New York City to lend what aid she could to her grandparents during their troubles. Star's arrival had coincided with the arrival of a gaggle of nurses to care for the invalids. "Your mother appears to be suffering from a temporary toxic psychosis, a reaction to some medication," said Dr. Clifford.

For true paranoids, Harry knew, "they" were often those closest to them. Dr. Clifford did, too, fortunately. So there was no need to fear that Estelle's mind was permanently derailed.

"I'm taking her off *all* medication for the present, in the hope of rapid mental and emotional improvement. When that happens, we can start giving her what she needs for pain, blood pressure and other problems—one drug at a time. At the first sign of renewed toxicity, we can withdraw the suspect drug and substitute something equally effective, but different in chemical composition. We have at our disposal at least a hundred and twenty-five different combinations of medications for high blood pressure alone, and choices enough for everything else that ails her."

His tour of inspection of Tom's wilderness completed, Harry came full circle back to the stile, climbed over it again, got into his ancient convertible, and drove to his parents' home. As he entered the front door he heard the cries.

"Help! Help!"

The wild cries seared him like a jagged flame of lightning, and he dashed upstairs toward their source. "Help!" He hadn't dreamed a human voice could project such terror through a closed door.

"I'm here, Estelle, I'm here! I'll have the door open in a second."

It would have taken even longer if one of the four nurses cluttering the upstairs hall hadn't had the presence of mind to bring up Tom's crowbar and hammer. Smiling, chummy Trudy—Trudy Campbell, the only nurse in the house who insisted on being called by her first name—had thought of this.

Still, it took more than seconds for him to hammer the crowbar between the door of the bathroom and the wall. The thud of the hammer blows mixed horribly with the screams that went on, and on and on.

Then the screams diminished. They ceased with the last thud of the hammer as if he'd hammered her skull instead of the crowbar. He dropped the hammer to the floor and leaned hard against the crowbar, calling in to her, "I'm coming, Estelle." The door began to give. Then his mother spoke with startling, unexpected calm. With something more than calm.

"Harry, my son." Her savior.

Harry leaned his whole weight against the door in a fury of impotence. Impotence against such mad faith. Doors he could handle.

"My son," she repeated weakly, but with the same total trust. Then there was the sound of something dropped or falling.

The door swung open, outward, toward him. Trudy took the hammer and crowbar and said, "Now we'll be all right. Our Mrs. Purdie will see to that."

The immediate realization that the huge bathroom was empty struck Harry like a fist. What was going on? He glanced feverishly from the big, cracked wash basin with an outsized, ornately carved wooden medicine cabinet above it, across an empty expanse of worn tiles to a high, claw-footed tub, its white enameled sides topped with a wooden rim that matched the wood of the medicine cabinet. Had he forced the door to an empty room? In response to unscreamed screams?

"Harry." The faintest whisper of absolute faith. A faith that made him squirm inside. Life, and death, would be easier if mothers didn't love so much.

Then he saw her, flat on her back in the bottom of the tub, in a faded blue nightgown. "Estelle! Are you hurt?"

24

"No. I just lost my balance and fell in. Get me out. It's cold here."

She reached up with one almost fleshless arm to him like, like—he tried to deny the resemblance as he bent to lift her— like his seven-month-old daughter wanting to be lifted from her crib. He gathered her up and felt her head drop against his chest like a baby's. Trembling, he held the emaciated body closer, cradled the trusting child, his mother.

"Take me away from here," she murmured, but without urgency, without strength.

A stronger voice at his elbow was babbling explanations. One of the nurses. And others. The upstairs hall between Estelle's room and the bathroom was still jammed with rubbernecking women. Ginelda, florid-faced and heavy, with iron-gray hair; and three nurses, two in uniform, and one in a flowered quilted housecoat. A second housecoat—Trudy's— had disappeared from the crowd. Maybe she'd gone to the shed to return the tools, someone said.

One of the uniforms sheathed a big-boned, handsome woman, with attractive brown eyes and neat brown hair. Usually she had a capable air about her, but now she appeared completely distraught. As she damn well should. His sister, Essie, had interviewed five nurses recommended by the registry and chose this one, Purdie, because she had a demeanor that suggested calm and competence. And, as his mother said, "She won't talk me to death." So how the hell had she let this happen? And why did Ginelda and the others stand there gawking? . . .

He turned savagely on the other uniform, Mrs. What's-her-name, Tom's day nurse. An old hen with a long, scrawny neck dripping wattles. "Get down with my father where you

25

belong! If he needed something, he could yell his fool head off and no one would hear."

"Yes, sir," scrawny neck said, scurrying to the stairs. "But I think we're resting quietly. We didn't hear the screams— that is, Mr. Morgan didn't because he was asleep with his door closed—and Trudy *did* go down to be near him the minute you dropped the tools."

"Never mind about that," he said to her hostilely retreating back. "Stay where *you* can hear him. That's what you're paid for. Don't forget it!" He hated her way of saying "we" when she referred to his father, but Tom didn't mind.

Still standing angry in the hallway, cradling in his arms his mother, who was unaffected by what he was saying to the assembled harpies, he half-shouted at Mrs. Purdie, "And why in hell did you let her lock the door?"

Mrs. Purdie's anxious face turned an ugly red, from rage or embarrassment, but she kept her voice low, courteous, full of concern. "We always *insist* on going to the bathroom alone. It's just one of our little ways, you know … "

That damn "we." They all seemed to use it, but it had never jerked at his nerves so much as now. "But when she's this weak and the place is lousy with nurses.… "

"I try not to cross my patients unnecessarily, especially when they're … uh … a bit confused. When the door— when she couldn't unlock it, she … she grew frightened. I couldn't reach her."

"Then she started a-screamin'," the flowered robe interrupted, wagging a be-curlered head of straw-like hair, dyed an orangy red. "Woke me right out of my sleep. Trudy, too." She nodded in the direction of the stairs down which Trudy had disappeared.

"And we was scared ourselves," another nurse spoke up, "knowing like we do what happened to Hettie. Anybody'll scare easy now. But we all come a-runnin' to help if we could, no matter *what's* a'goin' on."

"Except me," the bulging flowered robe said, swelling with importance. "I called Dr. Clifford and he's on his way. A good thing, too, seein' as how she fell. She could of broke something."

"I didn't," Estelle said softly.

"Very thoughtful," Harry forced himself to tell the flowered robe. Her breasts were shaped like oversized loaves of bread, yet the effect was not, as in some similarly endowed women, the nurturing, earth-mother look. "Go back downstairs," he said. "You too, Ginelda."

He'd have preferred to say, "Get away from here, you snooping bitches," but Estelle's remark had reminded him her featherweight body still contained a mind that understood English, and wasn't accustomed to hearing even the mildest profanities.

His using "hell" to Mrs. Purdie in his mother's presence, with her actually in his arms, was a slip that revealed how much he'd ceased to react to either Tom or Estelle as still alive, with the right to dictate the standards that would prevail in their own home.

The constant presence of Tom's three nurses didn't help either, scraped on his nerves. Not one of them ever went home for her off-duty hours. It wasn't worth it, they said, to drive back and forth to Louisville every day over twelve miles of icy roads. "We'd meet ourselves coming and going," Trudy said.

Tom agreed they were wise to avoid driving in this

27

weather, so that settled it their way. They lived here, ate here, gossiped here. Around the clock, like a coven of witches. All of them. Except Mrs. Purdie, who was of another breed. She commuted—one blessing to count—in an old Cadillac, her one extravagance, a dream made manifest despite the nattering of neighbors at her pretense. But like the others, her hovering and "we"-ing at his side irritated him just now.

"I'll stay alone with my mother for a little while. You wait out here," he said, indicating a small love seat by the front hall window. Then, pushing the door shut behind him with one elbow, he carried Estelle into her room, and laid her on the great four-postered double bed. She curled up on her side where the contours of the lumpy mattress had long since conformed to a shape comfortable for her, like a space shoe.

He sat beside her, wanting to know why she'd started screaming for help in the bathroom. He hoped she'd tell him, but was afraid to ask. He knew how extraordinarily dextrous she was with her left hand. She would have had no difficulty unlocking the door before the screams. Why had she locked it in the first place?

"Harry, you got here in time," Estelle said.

Such lacerating trust! "In time for what?" he asked, the words coming out of his mouth in spite of himself. Fight it though she might, she was going, going, almost gone. Like Tom. But Tom took it more stoically.

She patted his hand and replied, "With you here, I'm safe." He winced—imperceptibly, he hoped—and said, "You're safe anyway."

"With some people. You, Star. Others. I have to get it figured out—the trust list. When I'm not too tired." Her

28

eyelids closed. "You, Star, Tom, Essie . . . " and then she was asleep.

He left her to get the tools and materials to fix the bathroom door so she could latch it for privacy with a fastener. If necessary, Mrs. Purdie or anyone else could open it from the outside without creating any disturbance, by simply inserting a knife blade under it through the crack, and lifting. Outside, in the hallway, he told Mrs. Purdie, "See to it that no one mentions Mrs. Keller's murder again in my mother's presence. I don't think she got it this time, but make sure no one takes any more chances."

"Of course, Mr. Morgan. I'll warn everyone to take great care. Our nerves do need every possible protection."

Harry turned his back on her and descended the stairs, treading softly, as people do in a house where they know death is impending.

CHAPTER II

STAR BROKE FREE from a dream of having eaten succulent well-roasted flesh only to realize, after she'd swallowed it, that there was something revolting about it, that she might vomit. Even after she opened her eyes, the delicious flavor lingered on her tongue while her stomach continued to heave against some evil ingredient—arsenic? ground glass? what?— masked by the wonderful taste.

The scrambled impression of pleasure and rising nausea began to fade as she located herself in time and place. She was not in her room in her parents' New York apartment at 109th and Riverside. Or in her smaller room at Bard College. She was in the cabin, a former slave cabin long since remodeled into a guest house, some thirty yards from the back door of her grandparents' home. If she had to upchuck, the tiny bathroom was one step from the bed, but both the enjoyment of the dream—awake or asleep, she loved food—

31

and the aftertaste of nameless evil that imbued it had been dispelled with her full awakening.

Anyway, it would take more than a dream to upset her digestive processes. At the age of twelve, she'd gulped down a live cockroach on a dare, and though her conscience disturbed her afterwards—she was a card-carrying junior member of the A.S.P.C.A. at the time—her stomach did not. She wondered if she'd even have morning sickness when she was pregnant, and hoped she would—at least once—because she didn't want to miss out on anything in life, good or bad. But she wasn't pregnant yet.

She and George endorsed the sexual revolution wholeheart-edly, of course, but they didn't think it should be regulated by any set schedule. The old idea that girls should stay virgins until marriage was barbaric, but she felt a mandatory limit to virginity—late high school, early college, or what-ever—was just the same old Procrustean bed disguised in new sheets and she was having none of it.

Star had been a very late bloomer anyway, so physically and erotically retarded that only a short while back she began to fear she'd never bloom at all. A sad prospect for a girl who hadn't the slightest vocation to be a nun, wasn't even Catholic, but a reality she was stuck with until a certain moment this year, her eighteenth.

That moment—just three months ago—when George looked at her in the Bard cafeteria with an expression that made her know for sure she'd finally become pretty. Very pretty.

Oh, not beautiful. She'd never have a face that could launch a thousand ships, which was just as well since she was a pacifist, but George's gaze had revealed the fact that she could look forward confidently to loving, to having a man want her love, her cooking, her babies—one biological and some adopted. She didn't want to add to the population explosion. That is, not much. She'd have just *one* new baby, and several that were already here and had to be taken care of by somebody.

Meanwhile, she intended to stay a virgin until she and George were both sure they had reached the utmost pinnacle of mutual desire and trust. Then they would unite in their own time, in their own way, totally uninfluenced by the morals or timetables of any period in history.

At first, George had been reluctant to wait for this mutual evolution of feeling, but after a few days, he got a poster to hang over his dorm bed that ordered in huge letters: STEM THE RISING TIDE OF CONFORMITY. It showed her he'd begun to understand her point of view.

Her grandmother Estelle had understood it even more quickly when she explained it to her last week, the day she had arrived to spend the Bard midwinter work period as Estelle's night nurse.

"I grew up—got married—thinking sex without marriage happened only in French novels," Estelle had said, "or in something even more foreign like *Anna Karenina,* one of my favorites. But from what I read now—well, I'm glad you intend to hold out for more than just the safety of the Pill."

"Oh, I'll wait until I'm sure I hear the music of the spheres," Star promised, "until I know I'm floating on the Milky Way." And they both laughed, with a happy conviction that when they talked about love they were talking about the same thing. Something that transcended the customs of any culture or generation.

But that was a week ago. Another era. Conversations with

Estelle about love, literature, George's future (he was a senior, majoring in psychology)—anything that mattered—were now memories.

Star shuddered. She was unfashionably fond of both her parents and could even tolerate her twin brother Tommy, but she had always loved Estelle more than all the rest of her family put together. Since babyhood, she'd spent every summer of her life with her, and most Christmas and Easter vacations too. She was convinced that she and Estelle would have found each other congenial if they'd met recently on an airplane. But they'd met in Star's earliest infancy, and the bonds of natural congeniality had developed into a framework of love and trust, deeply sustaining to both of them. Until now.

Now the thought of being chained for years to an insane grandmother's sickbed frightened Star out of her wits. Sick with this fear and ashamed of it, she got out of bed to dress, dropping her nightgown, lacy and pink, to the floor. She hated the sight of it now that it suggested magic nights *not* in the cards for a girl who must sacrifice herself to a suffering lunatic. Unless she could bring herself to mercy kill. Which she couldn't. There was nothing in the cards these days for a girl who was devoted to her grandmother, except knowing that everyone, maybe even George, maybe even especially George, psychology major, would think she was a neurotic, getting a sick satisfaction out of the whole bit. Star began to cry, stupidly, helplessly.

CHAPTER III

THERE WAS A flutter of something alive in the dark crypt, among the cold statues of women lying on sarcophagus lids. Something that had to escape quickly, burst free of the marble dress they had carved too tight on her, breathe. That was it. She must breathe, breathe—her whole being struggled frantically for breath. Her wild terror swelled against the encasing marble, cracked its stone grip at last, raised her chest wall.

With the intake of air, a thought, a name, flickered in her brain. She attempted to cry out, "Tom!"

"Tom! Tom!" The cry didn't reach voice level but the charge she put into it lit flares of realization in the blackness of her panic. With tremulous caution, she moved her good arm up and down along Tom's side of the bed, pressing her fingertips against the strange, tight smoothness of the sheets— nurses made beds a lot better than she ever had—gaining certainty from the familiar lumps and hollows of the mattress on which she had first lain long ago, as a bride.

She was Estelle Morgan, wife of Tom Morgan, in the dark. There was a way to get out of the dark if she could remember how to do it. Then she did remember: if she opened her eyes, there would be light, or a light she could reach and turn on. There always had been.

After a shuddering hesitation, she raised her lids and saw her room, filled with late-afternoon sunshine. She was breathing freely, but they would try again. She would be able to scream aloud now if she wished, but Tom couldn't come.

Her terror receded a little, partially displaced by profound sadness. "My bow and quiver will rest in a corner, gathering dust." Those were the last words of an editorial Tom had written some months ago about conserving the natural resources of Kentucky. With an ache of sorrow, she repeated silently to herself the entire sentence of which the words were a part: "I fight in the way in which I am able and according to my light, but soon my bow and quiver will rest in a corner, gathering dust."

Now he couldn't write anymore, couldn't even walk. He could only breathe, and speak, and turn his head to look out at his trees from the windows of the sun porch. Stroke was the name for his sickness. He'd been struck down, as by a mighty blow. She could call and call and he couldn't come.

Even with the stairs a cascade of flames, Tom couldn't respond now as once he had, climbing up the oak tree to the roof and to their baby Essie's crib faster than the fire that burned ships in both wars, the one he fought in himself, World War I, and the other that came later when all those

Nazi submarines were looking for her son, her Harry, but Harry got himself home alive.

Then she'd had that maiming operation, long ago, with the searing pain, leaving in its wake a bad arm and the terrible flatness across her chest. But the flatness didn't matter too much when Tom touched her shoulder and said, "My wife, my lovely wife."

They would be easier to fight than fire or war or disease if she could tell him about them, about how they kept pushing her under again every time she nearly got it figured out ... before she ... no use; each time it was harder to come up through the blackness. They didn't intend to ever let her think clearly enough to get it straight. They were killing her in a way that would look like natural death, a way that would make people say, "It's a blessing she didn't last longer, with her mind gone." That's what they were doing, killing her by inches, mind first. But she would stop them. She was still alive enough, able to think enough for that.

Tom couldn't help her this time, but there were others who might. She checked an impulse to announce aloud to the shadows in the corners of her room: "I have a strong son, a man, a war hero, my Harry. He comes to see me every day."

Only how could she tell Harry or anyone what she didn't really understand herself? All she knew for certain was: they were slowly killing her. They ... they ... if only she knew who they were....

With a great effort she steadied herself against the trembling that shook her wasted body at the thought of their knowing that she didn't know, that she couldn't tell. Not even when they opened her dresser drawer and took the money from her purse right in front of her, in front of her and of the dresser mirror that reflected their every gesture as clearly as her own eyes, and yet was blanker now than her shattered memory.

She clutched her mouth with her good hand to avoid crying out at this horror, this knowledge that they were erasing her, secure in their confidence that they could keep her too confused to put the pieces of the puzzle together, to make anyone else understand what was happening.

She wasn't out of her mind. Not entirely. She could still remember a lot: the names of the two horses her father sold when she was four, Cinnabar and Cobbler; all she'd seen during a long, lazy trip down the Magdalena River in Colombia with Tom, when the children were both at college—but not what she'd had for lunch today, or even whether she'd had lunch. Nothing about today except noticing how tired Star looked early in the morning when Mrs. Purdie arrived and Star went off "duty" ... and ... and. ... The trembling increased as she strained to recall more and got nothing. Nothing more of today, or yesterday, or the day before. Tom! But he couldn't come. That much she did remember with aching certainty. She would always remember finding Tom in a pool of blood, on the bathroom floor, and how she couldn't lift him, though she hurt her back, cracked a vertebra, trying. Blood flowed from the wound where his head had struck the side of the tub.

We're dissolving together, my lover and I, she thought, and I don't mind too much. I don't mind dying, but Tom ... Tom ... don't let them murder me.

Her scream, shivering high and thin in the empty room,

connected with a surge of responding sounds: a rush of heavy steps and a jumble of voices downstairs, steps rushing up the stairs, steps hurrying down the hall outside toward her open door. Voices and steps closing in on her, none of them Tom's. If only she hadn't cried out, given herself away again. She closed her eyes tight against what was coming: the pain, the blackness, the end. The pain above all. Her every muscle tightened against it.

They were in the room, one of them at least. A strong hand gripped her right wrist. Her brain reeled at the agonizing pain, as someone forcibly straightened her bad arm. She fought back against nausea and dizziness. She must not faint. She must look, see, remember.

The hard hand released her wrist. She folded her burning arm back into the position that hurt least, elbow bent, hand resting on the collar bone. Quivering spears of pain radiated from it into every cell of her brain and body, blotting out everything else for a minute or minutes at a time.

Then she heard more steps in the hall, more of them coming. Tom—no, no—she mustn't scream. He wouldn't hear. Only *they* would hear, and do it again, and again. If she kept quiet, kept her eyes closed, they'd think she was dead. Nobody hurts the dead.

The pain lessened. Numbness rolled it back from the depth of her body and along the lengths of her good limbs. The numbness even mercifully reached the agony center in the crook of her bad arm, melting it as coffee melts a lump of sugar. There was a kind of bliss in this almost not suffering anymore.

But they stayed in the room. She could feel them leaning

bold and evil over her bed, waiting to hurt her again, if she opened her eyes. But if she did open them, she'd see who they were. She would remember. She would tell Tom.

No, not Tom. Tears welled up under her closed lids. Dear God, don't let me cry before them.

But that wasn't really what mattered. What mattered most was that the pain was gone, gone altogether. Only there was something else, something she'd forgotten but had known during the pain. She moved her arm slightly to summon an awakening jab against the enfolding languor, and remembered what it was she must do, no matter how great the cost. She must see them so as to be able to tell somebody if she woke again. Or if she didn't—if I should die before I wake— the surrounding presences were mother and father.

No—that wasn't it. She wasn't getting it right. She managed to move her arm again and opened her eyes. The tears that her tight-closed lids had been holding in blurred her vision a moment, then slid out of her way, onto her cheeks.

Then she saw them. She saw them at last, or again, great figures with blurred faces ghostly white in the darkening room, gathering round her bed, waiting for the rapidly increasing gloom to pull her back into itself. The faces were all scrambled, fading, splitting into two, but she focused on one until it congealed into a single set of features she recognized, a face with cold eyes that stared directly into hers.

There was a roaring in her ears, a roaring as of wheels that carried her swiftly away from it, from a face that grew smaller, smaller on a receding horizon but remained certainly one she'd seen before. It was the face of one of them, the one who had taken the money from her black purse.

That was what she must remember. That was her only hope—to remember the face and her black purse. The purse would be the way of recognizing at least one of them. The big black purse she'd had for many years now growing bigger, blacker, blotting out everything else.

CHAPTER IV

STAR CRIED A long time, until her grief and fear burned out and hope began to perk in her with the ebullience natural to her age. Estelle *did* seem alarmingly far out, but it was just a temporary condition; Dr. Clifford had practically guaranteed it. She was scared because of the way it felt being with Estelle at night now. Not because of any real danger that her grandmother had lost her mind permanently. Or could be scared half out of her wits for a good reason.

It would soon be time for her to replace Mrs. Purdie, Estelle's day nurse. She better wash her face and get some clothes on in a hurry. After dressing, she turned on the hot plate under her kettle to make coffee. While it was heating, she brushed her long dark hair carefully to a smooth shine.

When the last tangle was out, she spooned a generous helping of instant coffee into a cup, poured the boiling water over it, and carried it to a chair by the window looking out

43

on her grandparents' front yard, rimmed with great dark trees that threw clutching afternoon shadows toward the house from every direction, except for the twenty yards of fence entwined with grapevines, now dry and brown. In summer they would turn green again, their sun-warmed purple fruit bursting with luscious juice.

She sipped the coffee slowly and drifted into a daydream of sharing huge, sweet bunches of grapes with George, but in mid-fantasy she snatched at a cluster that was about to touch his lips, and at the same time stared in horror at the dry vines, thinking she saw a ghostly figure: first looming above the latticework, then moving menacingly across the yard toward the house. Perhaps Hettie Keller's murderer!

Then she saw that the figure was Harry carrying a bucket with which to fill bird feeders in the front yard. He looked strong, serene, the incarnation of everything safe and decent. A middle-aged farmer doing chores for his ailing mother and father. Seeing him as anything else would make her as confused as Estelle. And *she* wasn't crazy. But neither was Estelle, in any fundamental way.

Harry looked the same now as he had the day before yesterday, when he told her and Dr. Clifford about that horrible business of Estelle's locking herself in the bathroom. Star had been asleep here in the cabin when it happened, but the screams she hadn't heard seemed to echo now in her brain, though Harry and Dr. Clifford had discussed it all in a very low-key manner—probably downplaying the incident with her feelings in mind.

Since Harry still regarded her as a child, he'd naturally try not to upset her. Estelle believed strongly in providing serenity for children and gave her own and her grand-

44

children as much as she could, between Tom's roars. Harry and Essie accepted their mother's values, and Harry lived up to them with her and her brother Tommy, as well as with his own chidren. Essie tried to, but irritation often got the better of her.

"Everything still points to a toxic psychosis," Dr. Clifford had said. "But she hasn't had any medication for two days now. If my guess is right, her mind will clear up soon. Perhaps in another day or so."

"And if it—this psychosis—doesn't wear off?" Harry asked, while Star stood beside him, freezing, trying not to look scared, or cry.

"Then we'll be faced with a very painful situation indeed: paranoid senility. She does have *some* of the classic symptoms. I realized that when she whispered to me, 'They are trying to kill me,' but she couldn't identify 'they.' She got confused when I pressed her on the matter."

"And this can go on how long?" Harry asked.

"It *can* go on for years," Dr. Clifford said. "Institutionalization may become necessary."

"No," Star had vowed silently, "Estelle's life is not going to end in years, even months, of terror, alone in some asylum. No matter what *I* have to do to prevent it."

She knew asylum care could be good, if you pay enough for it, and that a brain may crumble into senility peacefully or even gaily. She'd seen one example this past fall when she and George, on a walk in the woods near Bard, had come upon a very old woman—obviously an escapee from some place—dancing all alone in a sun-dappled glade high above the Hudson, keeping perfect time to an interior melody, acknowledging the applause of an invisible audience.

For that woman, dancing against a backdrop of flashing scarlet-and-gold trees, there was happiness in insanity. But not for Estelle. As long as Estelle breathed, she would need to give tenderness and affection, in moments of lucidity, and receive it from her own family as well. Especially from her, Star.

Star felt trapped. She longed to live and learn and love freely; but could she ever, if it meant leaving Estelle alone in an unending nightmare? Estelle who had come running, so often and at all hours of the night, to soothe *her* childhood nightmares about the devil. And even earlier nightmares about something she called the ageegla-ageegla. Finally, Estelle's comforting arms had banished the ageegla-ageegla and Satan both, so thoroughly that they had not returned in other forms. And now. . . .

But she was jumping the gun. She'd been assured, almost promised, that Estelle would soon be in perfect shape again, except for the bad arm, which she claimed was arthritic. To prove this, Estelle always kept a book conspicuously displayed on her bedside table: *Arthritis Can Be Cured*. Star had grown up believing in this arthritis, waiting for the cure, until last summer when Essie, her mother, had told her the truth.

The arm withered thirty years ago after a very radical operation for breast cancer. Estelle hadn't wanted anyone but Tom and the doctors to know for fear her daughter, Essie, would think it hereditary and acquire it by auto-suggestion.

So Essie and everyone else had believed in the odd case of one-arm arthritis until about five years back, when Dr. Clifford, discussing Estelle's general health with Essie, mentioned the useless arm. Then, never suspecting Essie had been kept in ignorance for a quarter of a century, he had said, "Surgery for carcinoma can have that effect, if enough muscle tissue has to be cut away."

Essie had later told Star and Harry, but the cancer operation remained a family secret and Estelle never realized that the entire family had accidentally discovered the truth.

Estelle's left hand was remarkably competent. Star knew it always upset Essie and Harry to see Estelle—this frail-looking woman with only ninety pounds of weight spread over five feet five inches of height—alone in the big Chrysler, barreling along Highway 42 at sixty miles an hour or weaving rapidly through the heavy traffic of Louisville with only her left hand on the wheel, her right arm bent upward from the elbow as always, her useless hand resting on her chest. But she did it all the time with the aplomb (someone once said "the brassiness") of a confident cabbie, and never dented a fender.

At least she had until the night she found Tom unconscious in a pool of blood on the bathroom floor, six weeks ago, or seven. Nearer seven—from Thanksgiving to mid-January. A long time to stay sick, Star thought, even from the severest shock, to stay sick and get worse. She'd been worse last night, the second night without medication, than before. She had an accelerating illness. Dr. Clifford's words about possible senile psychosis rang in Star's ears.

"I'd rather see her dead than crazy," she said half aloud, with a sob. "I love her so much. Dead is better than crazy, than not being with it in anything but hurting."

She wiped her new tears with the heels of her hands, blew her nose, and turned her gaze from the lonely woods toward

47

the house to study a familiar feature of it that had become terrifying to her in the last few days: the pair of ladders, built onto the wall of the house, at each end, leading to windows in the two second-story bedrooms. She'd grown up thinking of them as providing safety exits in case of another fire like the one that had gutted the kitchen and dining room when her mother was a baby, and turned the only flight of inside stairs into a pillar of flame. But this week, for the first time, it struck her that the ladders could be used as a way of getting *in* as well as getting *out,* and she had guiltily locked all the windows of the house last night.

Tom would never have permitted such blocking of the upper-floor exits when he had been in charge. He would have sternly reminded her that the minutes, even seconds, lost getting a window unlocked, can mean the difference between life and death in a fire.

Fire and *cars? Who* could have wanted to kill Hettie Keller? Star had been questioned along with Ginelda and the nurses when she left her grandmother's bedside in the morning. Hettie's husband had come over to the Morgans with the police and Paul Ashton, and they didn't have a suspicion among them. It could have been a case of mistaken identity, as Paul had suggested. Someone killed Hettie thinking they were getting someone else. It seemed to Star the only reasonable possibility. She felt the police, and even Mr. Keller, thought so too.

But what a thing to happen. In Prospect, of all places. There'd never been a murder in Prospect before. Not since white men stopped killing Indians. Blacks had been lynched in Kentucky, but not around Prospect. But if murder could be committed in the Ashton driveway, it could be committed in the Morgan house, with the help of ladders.

The sound of a car starting down the hill, a horn dutifully blowing at the first curve, where a weathered sign commanded GO SLOW, LOOK OUT FOR CHILDREN, SOUND HORN, meant Harry's afternoon chores were finished. It was nearly time for Star to pay a brief visit to Tom and then replace Mrs. Purdie, Estelle's day nurse, in the sick room. But she had time to call her mother first. Not that she wanted to, but if she didn't, Essie would call her, and she preferred to talk here on the cabin phone. It had no extensions. So she dialed New York direct. "Hello," she said when Essie answered.

"How's it going?" Essie asked in a voice that begged for reassurance.

Star felt the muscles at the back of her neck contract with pity and anger. She knew Essie would already have called Harry and Dr. Clifford—she'd been calling each of them twice a day for a week—so why must she have the same answers a third time? Or rather, how could she reasonably expect her daughter to come up with anything new?

"I haven't been up to the house yet," Star said. "I haven't seen her since you talked to Dr. Clifford and Harry. I haven't heard a single scream out of her yet. She hasn't said a word to me about 'they' or 'them.' But she isn't logical all the time and there's something funny about her expression that keeps getting worse. It's been there for over a week now, in her eyes, as if she knows something I don't."

"Such as what?"

"I mean maybe she's trying to get help from Dr. Clifford and Harry. But not from me. Maybe because they're older.

49

Essie, do you think there's any possibility at all that she could be right?"

"Right about what?" Essie was genuinely confused. And no wonder. Star felt utterly foolish at the prospect of asking the question that nagged her mind, partly in the form of a hope—she'd rather Estelle dead than senile—but also in the form of a fear. A horrible question, either way. But she intended to ask it.

"Could she be right in believing she's about to be murdered—and not at all crazy?"

"Of course not! And the last thing she needs is for you to start imagining things!"

"Murder isn't something that happens only in my imagination! It's something that occurs in the outside world now and then! It 'occurred' to Hettie Keller the night before last."

"Darling, don't get angry. I didn't mean to hurt your feelings, but Hettie's tragedy has nothing to do with Estelle."

"Nothing except that nobody can explain it, any more than they can explain Estelle's fears. But I've been thinking—and I mean *thinking*, not *imagining*—that maybe some kind of criminal *is* trying to get at Estelle too. And I only *asked* if you'd thought of such a possibility."

"Well, I haven't. Neither has Harry, or Dr. Clifford. But now I will. Not that I expect to come up with anything. I mean, who on earth would want to hurt her? Except maybe Shad Traynor."

"Oh, my God! I'd forgotten Shad."

"Well, you can safely keep on forgetting him. He's in jail."

"Yes, I know. And even if he were to walk in the front door of the house right now"—the doors were locked but that

wouldn't slow up entry by a young man with Shad's talents—
"Estelle wouldn't be afraid of him."

"I know. She'll keep right on believing he's a poor,
mistreated child, really good at heart, until she actually sees
him come at her with an upraised meat axe!"

"Essie, don't! I'm going to be alone with her all night in
this dreadful wilderness!"

"Star! You've always loved the wilderness. And you won't
be alone. The house is full to bursting with nurses and
Ginelda."

"But they all sleep like death, and there are those darned
ladders at the windows."

"They're there, but nobody's ever come up them. The kind
of people who might, don't know about them, except for
Shad, and he's locked up. But if you're nervous, darling, I
could fly down. I don't want you to be under too much
strain. But Dr. Clifford is sure Estelle will be better soon.
Still, I could fly down. . . . "

"No, don't," Star said. "Tommy'll flunk his college boards
if you don't stay on his neck." Tommy was a year behind her
in school.

"And end up in the Army, I'm afraid," her mother said.

"I'm not all that nervous, Essie," Star said, determined not
to be responsible for Tommy's dying, or killing someone else
in a malarial rice paddy somewhere. Not that there was any
danger at present. But only a year ago, in 1961, Tom had
written an editorial warning against military aid to "our
Laotians" and predicting it would lead to real trouble for us
in Indochina before the decade was over. Poor Tommy could
be drafted whenever the "trouble" came.

"Well, if you need me, call—at any hour of the day or night. But there's really nothing to be afraid of."

"Of course not," Star thought. Less than two days ago, if Hettie Keller had expressed any vague fears, everyone would have thought that poor old Hettie was losing her marbles, exactly like Estelle, or maybe she'd just temporarily freaked out on aspirin, taken last week. But to her mother Star said, "I'll be O.K. Good night."

Shad Traynor! She could have done without being reminded of him. Estelle's greatest mistake. "Not good for anything, not even a tax deduction," Tom had once remarked, though not where Estelle could hear.

The Morgan household had become involved with four delinquents, including Shad, as a result of a dinner-table conversation that took place shortly after Estelle's inherited stocks skyrocketed into a fortune. It was at the beginning of the Christmas holidays seven years ago, and the whole clan was present, including Harry's young bride, Katinka, a Dutch girl, her first pregnancy barely visible.

Tom, inspired perhaps by Katinka's condition, started one of his diatribes on the dangers of the population explosion. He said it was regrettable that the natural rhythms of life could no longer be allowed to flow as freely as in the poetic days of Abraham, when it was ecologically right for the wife and the ewe to conceive and bring forth as freely as the flowers of the field. But unfortunately the wife must drastically control her reproductive processes from now on, though the ewes need not, since people can eat lamb chops, but not babies.

Put just that way, Estelle really understood the population problem, very likely for the first time in her life. And Tom, never one to stop a speech before the climax, added that instead of further depleting the earth's resources by producing more voracious babies, people should channel their nurturing instincts into caring for the surplus children already here, neglected and unwanted.

Estelle, ever eager to please her wonderful husband, took her first step in implementing this theory without further discussion. Tom had spoken. She had the money, recently inherited from her father. The Children's Center had neglected, unwanted children to spare.

Two days after this speech, Estelle went to Juvenile Court, taking Star along, and also Paul Ashton, her nephew-attorney, whom she'd asked immediately to locate four surplus children, neglected, unwanted, and in need of care.

Paul had located sad-faced, towheaded Shad Traynor at the Children's Center, waiting for his turn in Juvenile Court. He was the first of the quickly assembled group of boys that Essie sometimes referred to as "Estelle's baby cobras," though this really wasn't fair since only Shad had successfully resisted rehabilitation. At least the other three seemed to be doing well. They all lived within a few miles and had jobs and cars. Could one of them have gone bad and killed Hettie? For the sake of killing? Star tried to shake the thoughts out of her head. They were all good young citizens, now, except Shad.

The day Estelle acquired him, it was cold, wet and windy. The courthouse heating system had broken down. Everybody present was blue from the cold damp that crept up under the best coats. Star's thighs were all goose pimples and her hands were cold in fur-lined gloves. Shad didn't have gloves. A very undersized boy of twelve, he'd been arrested for the seventh time on charges of breaking and entering. He'd been nicknamed "Termite," because he was small enough to squeeze through grills and other openings too narrow for the slightly older robbers who made up the rest of his gang.

"May I express an opinion?" Estelle had asked the Juvenile Court judge.

He granted permission. Shad looked at the high ceiling and softly whistled the tune "Jimmy Crack Corn, and I Don't Care."

"With the assistance of my attorney, I have made extensive inquiries about Shad's background and difficulties," Estelle said, "and I believe he could be helped by a very fine treatment center I'd like to send him to. He'd get special guidance and care and remedial reading."

Shad, a confirmed non-reader with a truancy record dating back to the second grade, stopped whistling and glared at her as malevolently as if she had recommended the electric chair. But the judge was delighted to accept her offer to support him and three other boys in a tutorial school for disturbed and delinquent children run by a clinical psychologist.

"I'm still convinced it would have been wiser to invest in more gifted children," Essie would say any time the cobras were mentioned.

"I'm sure you're right," Estelle said, " 'to him that hath shall be given,' but there's something so pathetic about him that hath not."

Estelle collected her four have-nots in time to give them to Tom as a Christmas present. An envelope was hung on the tree, containing a fulsome account of their histories, and planned programs (including vacations in his home and wilderness). She said they were the foster sons for which he had so recently revealed a desire, in explaining how we should take care of children already here instead of having more.

Tom couldn't believe what he read. He made an inarticulate noise in his throat, blinked his eyes rapidly, and re-read; hopefully at first, and finally, expressionless. The second reading confirmed his dread that he'd understood the first time. For once he couldn't speak. Not for a long time. Finally he managed, "Thank you, my dear. You are ... *too* generous."

Later in the day, when Essie first used the phrase "Estelle's baby cobras," Tom ordered that each of "the young gentlemen should be made to feel welcome, every time he visits, by every member of the household." And so it was done.

Hopefully, the law would prevent further visits from Shad Traynor. Three hours after his discharge from the treatment center, he stole and wrecked a car. He had stolen two more since, and his most recent adventure got him a three-year sentence.

CHAPTER V

AFTER FILLING THE last bird feeder—his mother had six—
Harry drove to Prospect. Aside from the Prospect Store,
which was a grocery and social center for the residents of
surrounding farms for miles around, Prospect consisted of a
gas pump, a post office and eight residences, four of them
built in the last ten years, much to Tom's disgust. He didn't
like having a suburb bursting its seams a mile from his
wilderness.

Harry stopped at the gas pump and told a onetime class-
mate from the Ballard School, "Fill her up, and check the
oil, please."

While "she" was being filled, Martha Sneedon rushed out
from behind the cash register to the pump, yelling, "Mr.
Harry! Mr. Harry! You're wanted on the phone. It's Ginelda,
and boy, is she ever excited! Really excited!"

Harry rushed into the store and picked up the phone. "Yes, Ginelda?"

"Oh, Mr. Harry, I'm so glad I got you. There was a call for you just now. I thought you had ought to know about it right away."

"Who was it?"

"Shad Traynor!" Ginelda said, her voice full of fear and some pleasurable excitement at having such a piece of news to tell. "He got out of jail on parole today. A hour ago."

Harry groaned. Of all the things he didn't need to think about right now, Shad was at the top of the list. "What did he want?"

"He says he's outa prison on three years' probation and wants to visit here."

For the entire three years, no doubt, Harry thought.

"He says his probation officer give him permission."

That figured. One problem less for New York. Let Kentucky worry.

"I tole him we got no room and Miz Morgan's too sick to see anyone."

"If he calls again, just tell him to call Paul Ashton collect. You have Mr. Ashton's number?"

"Yes sir."

"Tell him if he really wants to come down here, Mr. Ashton can get him a plane ticket, round trip, and a hotel room. Then Mr. Ashton and I together will take him to see Mother. Meanwhile, don't say anything to Star. She has enough worries for a kid."

"No, sir, I won't." He didn't ask her not to discuss it with the nurses, being aware of the limits of her nature. The old biddies would enjoy endless speculations, both shivery and

58

titillating, about the chances of Shad's suddenly breaking into the house accompanied by Hettie's murderer and a whole gang of New York criminals.

To Harry, a visit from Shad, though a damned nuisance, wasn't quite the worst thing that could happen. It might give Estelle a lift. He returned to his car and drove home, remembering a bit uneasily the last time the Morgans had had any word from Shad. Not directly, but through someone else.

It had been some months back, a pleasant July evening, warm but not hot. His mother had invited him and Katinka to join her and Tom for their customary nightcap, a glass of sherry.

The drive from his home to the ancestral manse was lovely. The sky glittered with stars. The fields of his farm sparkled with matching fireflies. They found Estelle already in bed, but very much the happy hostess in a lacy, beribboned bed-jacket, her room fragrant with flower scents borne in through open windows.

Tom, still dressed, poured the sherry for Harry, Katinka and himself into tiny glasses, old wedding-present crystal. They all three sat in chairs drawn up close to the bed. Star, dressed in jeans, lay curled up on the bed, close to her grandmother, drinking a Coke and munching cookies.

The conversation had been about Laos. Tom told with glee how some of "our" Laotians disappeared into the jungle to do battle with Laotians armed by the Russians. Two weeks passed while anxious diplomats, American and Russian, waited tensely. Then our Laotians reappeared to report there had been no battle because one of their generals had been eaten by a tiger the first day in the jungle, so the two armies, "ours" and "theirs," made a truce for two weeks to give him a proper funeral, and then returned to their respective bases for a due period of mourning.

"Too bad about the poor general, of course," Tom said.

"Well, at least generals aren't an endangered species," Estelle said. "I hope the tiger escaped because—" She was interrupted by the phone on her bedside table. Harry, whose chair was near it, picked up the receiver and said, "Morgans' residence."

A voice with a startlingly vicious snarl in it answered, "Gimme the Old Lady!"

"I'll take the message," Harry said. "I'm her son." He didn't even want his mother to touch the phone with such a voice coming through it, though it came through loud and clear enough to be heard by everyone in the room. The Prospect phone system was in exceptionally good order that evening.

"Tell her to wire me a thousand dollars tonight. Send it to C. Clyde, care of Western Union, Grand Central Station, New York. One thousand dollars. I gotta have it for Shad Traynor's bail. And I gotta have it *now!*"

Before Harry could answer, Estelle reached out and took the phone from him. "I'm the Old Lady."

"Then wire me a thousand ... "

"I *heard* you say that to my son. There's no point in repeating yourself. I haven't any intention of sending money to you, or anyone else, for Shad."

"Look, Shad and me *need* the dough and you'll never miss it. So send it, if you know what's good for you."

"You're wasting your breath," Estelle said. "I won't be threatened."

"I'm tellin' ya—you'll be sorry. *Real* sorry."

Estelle hung up, without reply.

"I could *kill* him. Shad too!" Katinka cried.

"Katinka!" Tom exclaimed, in a tone so far short of his usual Jehovian authority as to betray a natural empathy for her viewpoint, though he felt honor bound to support his wife in her commitment to Shad.

"I myself wouldn't mind if Mr. Clyde met a Laotian tiger on its own turf," Estelle said. "He must once have been a sweet baby who could have turned out all right with proper care. Now he sounds as if all the good that was ever in him has already been destroyed. But don't *you* be upset, Katinka. He won't come here."

"That's right," Harry assured her. "Prospect just doesn't attract such people."

"What attracts his kind is money," Katinka said to Estelle, "and the chance to hurt, kill. I've known that kind of voice for years. And Shad's probably no better—'birds of a feather.' "

Estelle sighed. "I worry that Shad *may* be a lost cause, too, but only because he can't keep his hands off other people's property, especially their automobiles, even after almost seven years of psychotherapy ... "

"Which is for the birds, if you ask me," Katinka said.

"No," Estelle said, "the birds do very well without it. But it's a science that needs a lot of perfecting for the sake of people."

"I guess we can all second that," Star said.

61

"Anyway, Shad's only nineteen and his crimes have always been against property," Estelle said. "He's never hurt another human being."

"Not yet," Katinka said. "As far as I know, Hitler, Goering, and Goebbels hadn't killed anyone either at Shad's age. The worst criminals are sometimes late bloomers."

Well, Shad and his friends might be a threat for the future. This possibility would forever hang over the Morgan household, but if Shad wanted to see Estelle, there was really no reason why he shouldn't—for a few minutes, properly escorted by him and Paul.

As he pulled up to his own house, the front door flew open and Katinka ran wildly out to him. He gasped for fear she'd slip on the sleet-covered snow. She had no hat or coat on. The wind whipped her flying gold hair into beautiful disorder, and flamed her cheeks with red. Her full breasts, extra full because of her beginning pregnancy, curved outward against her bright-red sweater. The sight of her triggered a surge of desire in him. She was so gloriously alive and young. Seventeen years younger than he, too young for him, people often said. Or so he suspected. But with three babies and another on the way to absorb her energies. . . .

"Harry, Harry, Shad Traynor just this minute called. He wanted to speak to you."

"I know. He talked to Ginelda already—wants to visit Estelle."

She was nearer Shad's age than his, but of course she'd never be attracted to him, a confirmed thief—and possibly capable of worse.

"Did you tell him to call back?"

62

"No. I said you don't live here anymore, that you sold the house and didn't leave a forwarding address."

"Katinka!"

"I don't care. You Morgans don't believe in evil. I do. And I have three children to protect." She paused and ran her hand over her still flat abdomen. "Four children now. And I'm keeping Shad Traynor, C. Clyde, and such, away from this house any way I can. By shooting them from the windows if I have to."

"All right, all right. Don't get hysterical."

Of course, it was easy for him to talk. He'd fought the Nazis. Katinka had spent her childhood *living* under them with death always only a few heavy-booted steps from the door.

Harry put his arm around her, hoping to make her feel protected. "Don't worry about Shad. If it comes to that, I'll do any necessary shooting, but let's get into the house before you freeze."

CHAPTER VI

"Most of the day we rested very well," Mrs. Purdie said, "except for one bad moment. Nothing comparable to the fright in the bathroom the day before yesterday, but—a bad moment. I stepped out of the room just for a minute, when we were sleeping peacefully, to answer the doorbell. It was two friends—that nice Mrs. Thompson who's ninety years old, and Mrs. Levering. Both friends indeed to venture out in such weather."

"Yes," Star agreed. "At their age. But everybody loves my grandmother."

"Yes indeed. They left their cards and brought her some camellias. But I'd hardly opened the door for them when she screamed. We almost jumped out of our skins. All of us. I ran to the bedside as fast as I could, of course, and so did Trudy and Ginelda. Always butting in, the both of them, as if I don't know my business."

"I doubt they meant to imply . . . "

Mrs. Purdie interrupted her. "It was all over in a moment. Nothing like the bathroom incident yesterday. Just one cry. A nightmare cry. Trudy and Ginelda and the others came running . . . "

"As you said before," Star commented with mild boredom.

Mrs. Purdie drew herself up, seemed to expand in size like a blowfish on a hook. "I try to make things clear, for the benefit of my patient."

"Of course," Star said. "I'm sorry I was rude."

"One more thing," Mrs. Purdie said. "This morning she asked for her garnet pin. I searched everywhere. It's *not* in her jewel box or in any of her dresser drawers, or pinned to any of her dresses."

"Oh, well, it'll show up someplace," Star said, and went into Estelle's room. She studied her grandmother's sleeping face and resisted an impulse to smooth the sheet or adjust the badly misaligned blankets. Better let her rest undisturbed in a rumpled bed than risk waking her by trying to straighten it. The impeccable Mrs. Purdie must have reasoned the same way. Otherwise, she'd have neatened the bed herself before leaving.

"Sorry I was rude," Mrs. Purdie muttered to herself, in a fair imitation of Star's tone. "If I could get my hands on her, she'd find out what sorry *is*.

"Whore!" Still talking to herself, Mrs. Purdie unlocked the front door of her immaculate five-year-old Cadillac. "Like all the college kids today. Get everything handed to them. Never have to lift a finger. A garnet pin worth seventy-five, maybe even a hundred dollars, disappears and *she* doesn't give it a second thought. Oh well, easy come, easy go. Always more of everything for her kind. And look how they act. Look in the papers."

She turned the key in the ignition and started carefully down the hill. The smooth performance, the purr of the engine, quieted her nerves. As always, she felt more prideful driving this car—there's something you can't take away from a Caddy. It just has more to it than other cars, even after five years, or ten. That's why her Caddy was the only thing on which she resorted to physical labor—she spent hours Simonizing its already glossy surface. Though she could have afforded to have someone else do it—that was the kind of thing you could afford if you didn't have kids. Without kids, you can have more of everything. Even Karl admitted he was glad now they didn't have any, weren't stuck with something like Star. Though if Star were hers, she'd be different, all right. Mighty different. But that wouldn't make up for all the aggravation and doing without, as Karl agreed, one hundred per cent. Nearly every evening she read him a clipping from the *Louisville Times* about some kid gone wrong, a disgrace and an expense to the family, and he'd say, "You're right, Esmeralda. You were right from the beginning. We're so lucky we don't have *that* kind of problem!" Karl was right— no kids. Just a nice shiny Caddy instead.

Star sat down in a chair by the front window in Estelle's room and drew her feet up under the warm wool of her skirt. The chair creaked; then there was quiet. The only sound in the upstairs part of the high-ceilinged 150-year-old house was the soft bubbling of an aquarium, Harry's Christmas present to his mother, and the only light in the room came from the aquarium bulb, which extended its rays over the near side of the great mahogany bed, faintly illumining Estelle's sleeping face.

Emaciation had smoothed out many of the lines that had been part of that face since Star's first memories of it, and the underlying bone structure showed in a new way, making her look both infinitely older and strangely younger than she had in Star's lifetime. The pallor suggested the bloodlessness of exhausted dying, but the closer molding of flesh to bone revealed a startling beauty of structure. She was prettier than I am, Star thought. She was beautiful, long ago. Tom's beautiful Estelle.

Star's gaze fell on the aquarium and the small brightly colored tropical fish selected by Katinka. Above it there was a long shelf of black bound notebooks, each volume containing lists of Estelle's daily expenses for the past fifteen years.

The money so carefully accounted for was the income from stocks that Estelle's father had left her. For nearly a quarter of a century it had produced only a small quarterly income, when it produced at all. But in the late forties the capital and income began to escalate wildly, and seven years ago—the year of Estelle's cobras—it soared to a hundred thousand dollars a year, and stayed at that level, more or less, ever since.

"It's immoral, of course," Estelle had said to Star last summer. "There has to be something wrong with this Niagara of money pouring over me. If it were Tom's, it would make sense. He's worked hard all his life, with goals that matter—things your generation are just getting started on, like civil rights, and issues you still don't understand: population, pollution, the coming war in Indochina. But I've never earned a penny. Or even won a bingo game."

Star herself doubted the morality of unearned wealth, but it fascinated her all the same. This past summer, she'd read every page of the volumes over the aquarium, to Estelle's great amusement.

"What's so interesting about lists of daily expenses?" she asked. "You've never struck me as being the accountant type at heart."

"I'm not, but having a rich grandmother intrigues me."

"Nouveau riche," Estelle said.

"That's all right," Star assured her, "I'm not a snob."

Now she quietly rose and took the 1954 volume from the shelf. The early pages made dull reading. The one she was looking for came sometime in the fall. After a brief search, she found it in an early section of November.

Repair for washing machine	$ 8.90
Dr. Robert Clifford, for professional services	5.00
2 pairs of nylons	1.69
Hairnet	.15
Dr. Reilly Glore, for professional services to possum found on Highway 42, injured by hit and run driver, in need of surgery for internal injuries	32.86
First of five annual installments in a fund to establish a chair of conservation at a university of Tom's choice	50,000.00

Through the rest of the fifties and until nearly the end of 1961, Estelle had given away nearly all her income anonymously. The anonymity was partly to avoid the embarrassment of having so much more than Tom, and partly because Katinka dreaded anyone's knowing that the family was connected with serious amounts of money. She felt sure it would inspire some kidnapper to snatch one of her babies and kill it while Harry was following elaborate directions on where to leave the ransom money.

Star, unaffected by such worries, was more interested in the possum's surgery; according to a later entry, it recovered, snarling, every tooth bared. . . .

And suddenly she was stopped cold by the realization that Katinka might have a point. "Who could want to hurt her?" Essie had asked. The same kind of person who Katinka feared would kidnap her babies. Someone who wanted the capital that would be distributed when Estelle died. But that would mean Essie or Harry. They were the heirs, so there could be nothing to worry about.

Or *were* they the only heirs? Star hadn't read Estelle's will. No one had except Paul Ashton. There could be other beneficiaries. She could have included some creep, and even told him. The kind who would be in a hurry to collect, enough of a hurry to hasten her death. A far-out thought. But no more far out than Hettie Keller's death.

Star began to shake. Had Hettie died because of her visit to this house? She couldn't imagine any possible connection, but everybody was short on reasons for Hettie's murder. So Estelle could be right about impending danger in some unguessable form, slouching toward her sickbed from the woods, from the next room.

But this was absurd, of course. The next room was empty. The woods? Star turned in her chair and looked out the window. It still wasn't dark outdoors, and when night did fall, she'd be one of four able-bodied women looking after two sick people in a well-locked house. And there was extra safety in being twelve long, freezing miles from the slums of Louisville that had cradled Shad Traynor and the other cobras, with a wide belt of suburban and farm homes between. Lots of these homes belonged to very rich people, some richer than Estelle, and not one of them was entirely hidden in the depths of endless woods. Every last one of them was visible from some public road; more conveniently located for intruders than this, and more tempting. It comforted her to think how discouraged a wandering robber would feel, if he ever found his way here, after he'd cased the joint.

Tom and Estelle had never been ascetics, but for the last few decades they'd clung to the familiar, firmly protecting the belongings they'd collected during the best years of their lives from any changing touch of paint or repair, or from evidence of conspicuous consumption not compatible with Tom's salary.

If a burglar peered in the living-room windows, he'd see a horsehair-stuffed couch with some horsehair showing, an end table with a Scotch-tape-bandaged leg, two sturdier tables made by Harry in the ninth-grade workshop, a framed landscape painted by Essie the year she studied art, and comfortable chairs with unmatched hassocks, one of them embroidered by Star herself eight years ago. If he chose the kitchen, the sight of the holes in the linoleum might inspire him to leave a contribution on the windowsill.

The windless January dusk outside was intensely silent and cold. On her way to the house from the cabin, Star had

71

noted that the mercury in the back-porch thermometer had dropped to zero. It would go even lower in the night.

During the last few nights, no fox had barked, no owl hooted in the Morgan woods. In this kind of weather the dumbest beast, let alone a human predator, had sense enough to stick to its lair.

There is no safer place in the world than right here, she thought. Nothing bad can happen here except natural death.

CHAPTER VII

A GIANT TENTACLE groped blindly in the darkness for its prey, for her, was about to find her, encircle her in a deadly embrace, drag her into the darker darkness of its undersea cave. She swam harder, faster, up, always UP, through the black silence in which it sought her. The exploring tip grazed the length of her body, extended itself to coil around her. With a final effort, she shot up higher into a cleaner sea where it couldn't reach. It couldn't reach into the world of sound and light, where she was safe in a gently rocking boat with Star. Dear Star. So sweet and pretty even with those dark circles under her eyes, and that finger in her mouth. She must tell her to get more sleep. Must tell ... there was something else she must tell, must remember.

It would be easier to remember if she shut her eyes again but that would mean sinking back, down toward the waiting tentacle. There must be a safer way to break through the web of amnesia, woven so thick and tight around her by a human spider.

Eyes open, she tried to seize again the knowledge she felt she'd possessed a while ago in the dark, but it eluded her. Then she found she wasn't in a boat anymore. She was in her own room, with Star.

Money. That was it, or part of it. She'd been trying to remember something about money. She'd promised some to that nice woman who ... who ... something about a summer camp—crippled children. Essie used to love Camp Trail's End, and a song about the Tan Team girls with the rosy cheeks and the flying curls. Star's hair was straight, long and dark.

She shut her eyes and there was no tentacle and no darkness. There was a flowered field where children who had been crippled were now well and dancing in the sunlight.

But she hadn't given the lady the money for the camp. She had only pledged it and now the black purse was gone. They'd taken it and the money too, and they were going to kill her. That's why she must try to make someone understand, in time. An adult. A man.

"Star?"

"Oh, you're awake now!"

"Yes."

"How do you feel?"

"Happy that you're here."

But the speculative look in her sunken eyes was not happy, or encouraging to conversation. Star glanced at her watch. "It's six-thirty," she said.

"So late?"

74

"Yes. You've had a good long nap. I'll ring for your supper."

"I am hungry."

That's a good sign, Star thought, and pressed the bell to make sure of its being heard above the yakety-yakking that always went on in the kitchen between Ginelda and the nurses.

Estelle looked at the aquarium. "Have you fed the fish?" she asked.

"Oh, no, I forgot. I'll do it now."

"I like the little black one best," Estelle said. "He looks like a scrap of velvet come alive."

"Very alive," Star agreed. "I think *he's* pregnant."

Estelle's face brightened. "Oh, I hope so."

Star smiled, feeling encouraged that her grandmother could still care about the birth of fish. As she was sprinkling the fish food over the bubbly surface of the aquarium water, she heard the sound of heavy steps on the stairs. Ginelda was coming with the supper tray.

Estelle touched Star's hand lightly and said, "Don't leave me alone with her. I *think* I can trust her, but I'm not sure. Just a little afraid that ... " Her voice trailed off into an incomprehensible murmur.

"Of course you can trust her, but I'll be right here."

It was the first time she'd said anything to Star about fear. She said it in a calm tone, but it gave Star a feeling of having melted ice in her blood. She couldn't see herself, but she suspected her expression must have revealed the dismay she struggled to repress, and knew there had been a tremor in her voice when she answered. Even an ordinarily insensitive person would have noticed, would have asked her what was the matter, but Estelle didn't. The mad have no awareness of the feelings of others. Of course, the deeply, legitimately preoccupied can be equally unresponsive, at times.

As Ginelda's ponderous steps continued their slow approach, Estelle sat up, unsupported for a moment and as straight-spined as usual, while Star arranged a bank of pillows for her to rest on while she ate. Star worked as quickly as possible, trying not to pay too much attention to the emaciation that had occurred in the past few days. Her grandmother's spine stood out under the faded blue gown like a ridge, jutting half an inch beyond the barely covered ribs on either side. It was amazing that she could still sit unsupported at all.

"You can lean back now," Star said, as she placed the bed table across her lap.

Ginelda entered. The expression of her pale-blue eyes was sullen as she came through the door facing Star, but when she turned toward Estelle she broke into a loving smile. "Now, Miz Morgan, I got a real nice dinner for you. After that good rest you done had today, I just know you're right hungry."

"I am," Estelle said. Ginelda laid the tray on the bed table, then loomed over Estelle, her heavy florid face almost touching the skimmed-milk-pale one against the pillow, her wide mouth exuding a lot of breath along with loud endearments. "You're looking real good, hon," she lied. "Now just let your Ginelda fix this here pillow the way you like it. There! Your Ginelda knows how to take care of you, don't she, hon?"

"Yes, yes," Estelle said.

"Well now, hon, anything you want you just call your Ginelda anytime. You know I'll be right here. You know I done promised you I'd stay with you until you die, and I will. There ain't nothing I wouldn't do for you. You know that, don'tcha, hon?"

"Yes, Ginelda, yes."

"Well now, then I'll just go down and leave you to enjoy your supper," Ginelda said.

Star kept her back turned, pretending to be absorbed in watching the fish eat. When she had tried to tell Ginelda to stop talking to Estelle about dying, she'd found herself fighting not only Ginelda's obstinacy but also a supporting hostility on the part of Tom's nurses. "Bosom friends," they and Ginelda called each other. "Ginelda's been an angel to Mr. and Mrs. Morgan," one of them would inevitably announce.

"A real angel to the both of them," another would insist. "They'll probably leave her enough in their wills to take care of her for life."

When the angel had clumped downstairs, Estelle said with an uncertain smile, "Sometimes she gets so affectionate I feel as if she were about to eat me."

Star turned away from the aquarium and pulled up a chair close to the bed. Ginelda had placed a tiny slice of rare roast beef, a small salad of lettuce with two cherry tomatoes, and a glass of milk on a large silver tray. Star knew that the underside of the tray was engraved with Estelle's maiden name and wedding date: Mary Estelle French, February twenty-third, 1909.

The border of the tray was very ornate, a bacchanalian design of plump silver grapes hanging from thick vines among leaves that seemed blown by a summer breeze. A border definitely designed to suggest worldly delight, which reminded Star of various phases in her life—as when she was almost ready for college and eschewed the riches symbolized by the ornate tray. And of a religious phase in her childhood when she spurned her family's agnosticism and decided to embrace the Bible Belt Fundamentalism of the Prospect Baptist Church and become a saint. Of course, saints weren't mentioned at the hard-shell Prospect Baptist Church, but Star had read A Child's Garden of Saints, and had visions of herself dying young and pure at the stake, clearly seeing heaven above the consuming flames.

That religious phase happened the summer she was eight when, on a rare visit to church with Estelle, she heard a vivid sermon on hell-fire. It had so terrified her that she realized once and for all she wouldn't enjoy living in a garden of saints when other people were being roasted alive, day and night, forever. So the system of "saved" and "not saved" simply had to be changed, and in a flash of inspiration, she realized how to do it, with help. She got five other children, three blacks and two whites, to agree to meet her secretly every day all summer at the far end of the Morgan grape arbor and help her end evil forever.

Her plan was simple. They would dig a hole straight down into hell, let the poor sinners out—they could all go right down to the Ohio River and cool off—and catch the devil and roast him and eat him.

Did that planned feast of long ago have something to do with what she had dreamed this afternoon of having eaten luscious-tasting flesh tainted with evil? She wasn't sure.

When later Tom had found a six-foot-deep hole at the

bottom of his grape arbor, he explained there was no hell and that evil wasn't a devil with a tail. It was something in people.

Star shuddered again and looked at her grandmother. If Estelle was preoccupied and not insane, if she was thinking about a real danger, what were the possible answers to Essie's question, "Who could want to hurt her?" No one, of course. Just as no one could have had a reason for driving a car back and forth over Hettie Keller's body.

Essie had said "hurt." She hadn't been able to say kill or murder. For Star, words didn't matter. All that mattered was: What could *she* do face to face with a determined killer? Try to kill him first, of course. But how? How do you kill people when you haven't had any practice?

She was scared. For an agonizing moment, she wanted her mother. With a child's desperate, frightened kind of wanting. Then she remembered she was eighteen, a college girl. "Excuse me a minute," she said to Estelle, "I want to make a phone call."

"Go ahead, darling."

She went to the back bedroom, plugged in the phone, and called George in New York. She had meant to explain carefully, but at the sound of his voice, she blurted out, "Can you fly down here? Now! Tonight."

"What for, for God's sake? I'm in the middle of my thesis, the hardest part."

"You can work in the cabin." She burst into tears. "I need you! I'm scared!"

"What is it?"

"My grandmother thinks someone is out to kill her. I think she may be right. If she is, I'll need help."

"I'll catch a plane down tonight. I'll be there before dawn."

"Please," she was still crying, "take a taxi from the airport to the bottom of the hill. But *walk* up the hill. Bring a flashlight and go into the cabin. It's unlocked. I can phone you from the house if I need you in the night, but don't let anyone see you. Tom wouldn't approve or understand."

Now she wondered why she'd waited—maybe she wouldn't live long enough for it to happen. "Love postponed is death," she thought with slightly romantic terror. Had she made that up, or read it somewhere?

CHAPTER VIII

ESTELLE LOOKED BETTER, more alive, after she had eaten a little roast beef, all her salad, and drunk the entire glass of cold milk; but she also looked neglected, like a patient in a county nursing home who has outlived any friends or relatives who ever cared about her. Star had smoothed the sheets, straightened the covers, brushed Estelle's white hair, and tied it back with a blue satin ribbon. But the freshness of the ribbon and the neatness of the bed accented the dinginess of the faded nightgown.

"Harry and Katinka will be coming over to see you very soon," Star said. "Don't you think it would be nice to put on a clean gown for them?"

"No!" Estelle cried, as if Star had threatened her. "Please, no."

"Whatever you say, of course, but ... "

"Tomorrow, maybe. Not tonight. It's not really soiled. I don't want to change it."

"Then we'll wait," Star assured her uneasily. She'd been waiting three days already.

All of Estelle's gowns were ankle length, with high necks and very loose kimono sleeves. She'd had half a dozen made to order in this style, several years ago, designed to conceal her chest and upper arms. Until this week, they'd been very satisfactory. But in the last few days, Estelle's body had become strangely rigid, as though constantly tightened against something. This had made changing gowns, pulling them over her head and bad arm, very painful the last time Star had succeeded in doing it. That was three days ago.

The idea of going through the same struggle again, with her grandmother's body more taut than before, was dismaying. But she also hated to see Estelle, normally a dainty person, looking so unfresh.

"Instead of changing the gown, you could sort of cover it," Star suggested. "Put something on over it. The white satin negligee Essie got you for Christmas would be easy to get into. How about trying it?"

"No," Estelle said, with a vagueness that indicated she wasn't really aware of owning a new negligee.

"It's about the prettiest I ever saw," Star said.

Estelle didn't appear to have heard, so Star gave up.

A horn sounded in the distance, and Estelle's face lighted up. "Maybe it's Harry," she said. "I hope they bring Rachelle."

"*Rachel*," Star said, knowing it was hopeless. Katinka, several years younger than her compatriot Anne Frank, had decided all her children should have Jewish names, in memory of the victims of the Nazis. The name of the oldest, Sarah, was no problem to Estelle, but she objected to the next being called Naomi, feeling that Ruth was more attractive. And Rachel was always going to be Rachelle to a grandmother who had spent her honeymoon in Paris.

Katinka had stood firm on keeping Naomi from becoming Ruth, but gave up on the Rachel-Rachelle issue when her mother-in-law asked, "What have you got against naming at least one child in honor of the murdered French Jews?"

"They're here," Star said, "and they did bring Rachel."

Estelle adjusted her hair ribbon and pulled a corner of the bedspread over the thin shoulder against which her hand lay clenched into a small, shriveled fist.

Steps were heard on the stairs—Katinka's high heels tapping, followed by Harry's slower, heavier tread. Katinka came in first with Rachel in her arms. Then Harry entered and leaned down to kiss his mother.

"How are you, Estelle?"

"Fine." She looked thoughtfully at each face in the room: Harry's, Katinka's, Star's, Rachel's. Rachel smiled, displaying her new white teeth, both of them. "So safe, with you—all people I can trust."

"There's no one in the house you can't trust," Harry said.

Star glanced at Katinka, still just inside the doorway, and got a sharp impression that her own doubts were shared by her aunt. Or did she only imagine that a certain wariness, habitual to Katinka, was newly heightened?

"I'd like to hold the baby," Estelle said.

Katinka laid Rachel on the bed in such a way that Estelle could cuddle her in her good arm.

"Let's have some sherry," Harry suggested, and started

toward a small mahogany table where there was a silver tray with a half-full decanter on it, surrounded by several small glasses, their crystal prisms reflecting the bed-table light.

"No!" Estelle cried. Harry stopped short and turned to look at her, startled and perplexed.

Star saw now that Katinka's feelings were more nearly like hers and Estelle's than Harry's.

"That decanter could have been tampered with," Estelle said. "You remember the Medicis—"

"They've been dead and buried for hundreds of years," Harry said.

"I know. And not one of them ever set foot in Prospect. So if they're not resting in peace, at least they aren't roaming about among our trees, but remembering them has helped me with something I've been trying to get in my mind's grip—my black purse. It had all my money in it."

"Most of your money is in banks," Harry said.

"You remember you got me three hundred dollars from the bank, Harry. Before Christmas."

"Yes. You didn't say why you wanted it. Maybe you should tell me now what you wanted it for."

Estelle seemed to no longer hear him, or see him. "I was in a berth on a train hoping they wouldn't do it, but they did. Then I saw the face."

"What face?" Katinka asked in a tone of such urgency that Rachel stopped smiling. Terror is as contagious as the black death, Star thought. Even an infant can sense something of it.

"The face of one of *them. The* one—the one who took my black purse from the top of my bureau." She spoke slowly, with cautious, intense concentration. "I know I haven't been on a train for several years, and I can't remember what I didn't want them to do, but you can see yourselves that the purse is gone." That fact was a slight rip in the tight veil of amnesia they'd shrouded her in. "Essie put it on the bureau before Christmas, but it isn't there now."

They all looked at the bureau. "It must have got mislaid in the hurly-burly at Christmas," Harry said. "This has never been an organized household, with a place for everything, and all that."

Estelle, relieved, as if she'd told them what they needed to know, looked happily at Rachel.

"It's like having Essie in my arms again," she said. "Or Harry, or Star. Inside, I'm the same me that rocked my own babies and snuggled in my own mother's lap. She had a long, green dress and a dog bigger than I. A St. Bernard named Hector. That was in another century."

She remembers her mother's clothes and the name of a dog in the 1880s, but the mention of the negligee Essie gave her for Christmas doesn't ring a bell, Star thought, and she very likely has already forgotten what she had for dinner, or whether she has eaten at all.

Estelle was very quiet after Harry and Katinka and the baby left. Not sleeping, but disinclined to talk. Her expression was more reflective than tense and Star began to feel a responding relaxation in herself. The withdrawal of the drugs must be beginning to have a good effect finally. The improvement Dr. Clifford had expected seemed to be happening. The terror of the last few days was turning out to be only a bad dream after all.

Star leaned back in the cushioned chair in which she sat and allowed herself the luxury of closing her eyes. If she did go to sleep, a word, a whisper, from Estelle, would be enough to wake her instantly.

She's lovely in sleep, even with her finger in her mouth, Estelle thought, looking down at Star. Such lovely eyelashes, dark on a soft cheek. She's how old now—sixteen? Seventeen? Around that, but she still looks like a little girl, vulnerable. Sleeps like one too, like a tired child. Essie used to sleep so hard when she was small that she could fall out of bed and not wake up.

For a moment she almost saw her babies very small in warm blue pajamas with feet in them. If she could go back to then—but you can't go where you want in time, backward or forward, as you can in space, a house. You can go from one place to another in a house, if nobody stops you. There was nobody to stop her now, if she went quietly enough, didn't wake Star, didn't let *them* hear her.

She felt a little unsteady. She hadn't walked much since . . . since whenever they started destroying her, except to the bathroom and back. But she would manage. "Where there's a will, there's a way," her father had frequently told her. Miss Reilly, too. Rose M. Reilly, principal of the Ballard School, where Essie and Harry went, who always said "crik" for "creek" and "Where there's a will, there's a way." Essie had been Queen of the May the year she graduated from Ballard, and had lots of will.

Will. She took three steps very quietly and reached the dressing table. Her reflection in its mirror wasn't very clear, but she could see enough to know she should have let Star change her gown, no matter how much it hurt the bad arm. But Tom wouldn't care. He'd never paid much attention to clothes. It wasn't how she looked that mattered now. What mattered was that he should know she loved him. Know he wasn't dying downstairs forgotten, with only nurses. Know it now, before it was too late for her to tell him. Before they finished killing her.

She must touch him, tell him. Make it a kind of wedding. They had had a wedding at the beginning. They must have one now at the end, be joined together, in sickness, and for worse, so as to help each other remember the way it was in the good young years.

Young is good. That poem, "Grow old along with me, the best is yet to be"—that was what Tom would call "poppycock." The best wasn't yet to be, but at least it had once been. Remembering it made walking easier. She started moving again, feeling that the memory of the best was something she could hold on to as she went toward Tom. It wasn't as if she had to go far. There was just this hall, the stairs, the dining room, the little back hall, the kitchen, and then the sun porch, where she'd be with him. As she would have been every day of his illness if they hadn't— But she mustn't think of them. Memories of them weren't the kind she could lean on. She had to grasp the hall chair with her good hand to steady herself against thinking of them.

The chair was near the door of a closet—or was that the hall door? She let go of the chair and opened the door. It was the closet where her best clothes were kept. Everything seemed to be there still: The smoke-blue suit she'd bought last time she visited Essie in New York. The beige cocktail dress—she didn't remember that. A yellow dress—or was that a coat? Things began to blur. And then ... something else ... it looked new, beautiful, gleaming white. She touched it. It was satin.

White satin—a wedding dress. It was as beautiful as the

one she had for her wedding, and it opened down the front like a coat. It must have been made that way so she could get into it without help, or too much pain. She would put it on when she got to the foot of the stairs. It was too long to walk downstairs in. Might make her trip. She'd have to carry it down and put it on in the dining room. Once she and Tom had made love on the dining-room floor, and he called her his moss rose. That's what he often called her. At first, she only half liked it, would rather have been some corsage flower. Maybe an orchid or a gardenia. This was because of having been brought up near Rittenhouse Square in Philadelphia instead of near Blue Branch Creek in Crittenden County, like Harry, her son. He dressed up like an Indian and, looking fierce, on the Ballard School stage, had recited "Kentucky means dark and bloody ground." Then the rest of the fifth grade joined him in singing:

> Gee but I'm lucky
> That I'm from Kentucky.

She finally reached the stairs, got down three steps and had to stop, clinging to the bannister and trying not to drop the wedding dress. In dreams she often floated downstairs—up, too, her feet never touching the steps. But this was different. Her feet must touch every step between her and Tom.

She managed another four steps and stopped again. The weight of the wedding gown hanging on her arm made the going difficult. But where there's a will. . . .

Star had once gone to bed alone in a hotel room and awakened late at night to terrified awareness that she was no

88

longer alone. In the hotel her screams had rent the night, and other guests had succeeded in rescuing her from the light-fingered invader who wanted money, jewels, and probably her. A similar terror gripped her now at the realization that she *was* alone. *No one* was breathing or moving near her in *this* room. Before she opened her eyes, she knew the great mahogany bed was empty, that the whole upstairs was empty. The absolute silence proved there was no one—no one alive—in this part of the house, except Star herself.

She got to her feet with difficulty, feeling as she sometimes did in a nightmare, when she wanted to scream but could make no sound, wanted to run but was leaden-limbed. She grasped for a second the idea that the nightmare sensation meant she was in fact dreaming, that the incredible absence wasn't a reality. But she was awake. The bed was empty. The room was empty. She would search the rest of the upstairs and find nothing. Or a corpse.

She searched the few places where Estelle could have fallen, and the places where "they" might have stuffed a body. Then she started for the stairs no longer searching, intending only to wake the household, call the police. As she looked down the stairs, she became aware of something: a pool of white below, all the way down. Then she started screaming, knowing that the screams that had scared off the intruder in the hotel room wouldn't animate the thing at the foot of the stairs, but still not able to stop herself.

Someone was shaking her. It was Ginelda, ordering her to shut up, asking, "What's the matter? You crazy?"

She was now at the foot of the stairs, not knowing how she had got there, standing where the white had been, but it was gone. The only white visible was that of the uniforms of the nurses gathered about.

"Estelle fell down the stairs! I saw her lying there—here—"

"Hallucinating," one of Tom's nurses said.

"I saw—I saw!" Star screamed.

"You saw this here," Ginelda said, showing her something white. "The fancy robe your mother give her for Christmas. It was on the floor at the foot of the stairs."

It was the negligee, only a negligee. But the bed upstairs was still empty. "She's gone," Star cried, "go see ... see ... see!" They'd all have to see. She couldn't tell them.

Only Trudy ran up to see. Ginelda ran the other way, and a moment later, called out that she'd found her: She was in bed with Tom, lying on top of the covers. His arms were around her.

"I only left him a few minutes," his night nurse said, "just to go into Ginelda's room ... "

"That's all right," Estelle told her. "Very considerate. We wanted to be alone, and I wanted to wear that"—she pointed to the negligee on Ginelda's arm—"but I dropped it. My wedding dress. Put it on me now."

"We have to get you back up into your bed," Star said, between wrenching sobs.

"Don't cry, Star. Weddings are happy. Now put the dress on me." She stood up and looked expectantly at Ginelda, and at Trudy who had just returned nearly out of breath.

"Humor her!" Trudy whispered. "When we want to wear our bridal gown, we must be allowed to wear it."

Ginelda hung the shining white robe on the sick woman's shoulders.

"Beautiful," Tom said. "I love you, Estelle."

Estelle nodded. "That's it. That's the way it was. Will be. Love and cherish. *They* won't stop me from cherishing. Not anymore. I'll stop *them*. Where there's a will, there's a crik-creek. . . ." She swayed and half fell against Ginelda. Ginelda caught her and picked her up.

"I'll call Harry to come over and carry her up the stairs," Star said.

"No need of that. I can do it myself easy. She's about asleep in her Ginelda's arms already."

Star followed the big woman up the stairs with, for the first time, a liking for her, a feeling that here was strength and capability she could lean on, and she ached with the need to lean.

"Will you stay with her a few minutes while I get something for a headache?" Star asked after they had settled Estelle comfortably in her bed.

Estelle half raised herself from the pillows, but Ginelda pushed her back down caressingly, and there was no resistance. Estelle looked imploringly at Star but didn't say anything. Ginelda murmured soothingly, "Of course, her Ginelda'll stay with her. Now you just lie still, hon. You done had a hard night. You need a good rest."

Star left the room shaking; she was exhausted, and her head felt as if it were about to shatter into a thousand pieces. She had to do something about herself, and quick. Take something to ease the pain in her head.

She went to the bathroom medicine cabinet, but it was empty. Then she remembered she and Mrs. Purdie had agreed that all the prescriptions and medications, new and old, should be put out of Estelle's reach so she wouldn't take anything, not comprehending she shouldn't. They had collected numerous bottles of pills and capsules into two shoe boxes and stuck them on a high shelf in the back bedroom closet. Star climbed up on a chair to get down one of the boxes. She had to ease the pain that was cracking her skull. She fumbled among the bottles looking for aspirin. There were so many bottles—Seconal, Demerol. It crossed her mind that the Demerol bottle had been full—she was sure it was just two or three days ago. Now it wasn't. Same with the Seconal. What would—? Who—? She tried groggily to collect her thoughts.

She swayed and the chair tipped dangerously. She grabbed for the clothes bar with both hands to keep from falling. The chair steadied. She stepped off it. The shoebox slipped from her hands and the medicines scattered all over the floor of the dark closet. Except for one bottle. The aspirin! It had landed in the room, on the rug.

She picked it up and swallowed two tablets without water. Then she took a third and sat on the bed to wait for results. Just sitting quietly instead of standing was a help, plus the triple dosage, Star convinced herself. Sit a while longer . . . maybe the horrible pain would subside a bit. She lay back, put her head on the pillow, her feet on the bed, and shut her eyes. No voices to undo the relief she was beginning to feel, no one else in the room—a fiery pain pierced her head again as she recalled Estelle's plea, "Don't leave me alone with her." Star started to rise and then fell back on the bed. "Just hallucinating," she said to herself, as the nurses had accused her of doing at the foot of the stairs. Another mad thought passing through poor Estelle's mind, that's all. Why, Ginelda had been with Estelle for years; of course she could trust her. For five minutes more at any rate . . . the pain was easing . . . give it a few minutes. How she wished for George; he's probably landed by now, perhaps already making his way with his flashlight up the dark, silent hill. She hoped he remembered to wear warm clothes, a heavy overcoat, wool gloves ... warm things ... warm as she was now. Oh, the blessed relief in her head ... thank goodness for this nice warm room.

Everything was silent as the warmth and heavy sleep enveloped her.

CHAPTER IX

SHAD TRAYNOR HESITATED; there was something familiar about the woman up ahead. He'd seen her before—if he could only get a closer look. . . .

The woman disappeared into the airport cocktail lounge. Shad thrust a stubby-fingered hand in his pocket to check on his wallet. It was there, good and thick. He could follow her—this is a free country, if you have money and look square.

And one thing he'd got out of that school Estelle stuck him in was the Snyder technique of passing for square. It came natural to Dr. Snyder, a young psychiatrist, but Shad had carefully learned to imitate it: the various expressions, tones of voice, and ways of moving, the whole bit. Even some of the vocabulary. It hadn't solved all his problems, but it went a long way with policemen, judges, parole boards, probation officers. They all tried to go easy on a clean-cut boy who knew when to say "Yes, sir," and knew how to get a concerned, trying-to-understand look on his face when they questioned him, and then admitted only what they already knew, with an air of a sadly repentant young man who had made a mistake, but could not tell a lie. Shad, the cherry-tree kid. A little overgrown for the part but still young enough to give hope to would-be rehabilitators.

His own hope was to become the best cat burglar, bank robber, and escape artist in the whole United States. Famous as Willie Sutton, or the Thief of Baghdad. But this wasn't the moment to advertise it.

He changed his stance a little, getting the slouch out of it, and entered the cocktail lounge, using the Snyder stroll. There was nothing better than the Snyder walk for making a burglar look as honest as your friend at Chase Manhattan.

"Scotch on the rocks, please," he told the bartender in his best Snyder voice. Then he turned on the stool to get a better look at the woman. Christ—it was her! Tom Morgan's daughter—Essie! She was sitting at a small table hardly six feet from him. If she turned her head just a little his way, she'd be looking right at him!

She must be going to Louisville too. Maybe he should offer to sit with her, keep her company on the flight down. She'd love that. The Morgan kids loved him like they would the clap. They and Katinka, too. He smiled at the memory of Katinka telling him over the phone in that Dutch accent of hers, "Harry Morgan doesn't live here anymore, sold the house—no forwarding address."

A waiter removed an empty double-martini glass from in front of Essie and set a full one in its place. She stuck two fingers into it to get the olive out. Bad manners. But you don't have to think about things like that if you're a Morgan.

She looks good, he thought, and to manage that, she has to try plenty at her age. Dyes her hair and probably hasn't had a real meal in years, but you got to hand it to her: the way she's hung on to her figure, she could still make out as a hustler. Not in a first-class place, but Mom Jenny'd be glad to have her. Katinka, of course, could start at the top and stay there for a while. Quite a while.

Shad watched Essie take a small bottle from her purse and lift off the plastic top. He was near enough to see the two small orange capsules she carefully poured into her open palm. He saw her wash them down with big gulps of martini. Slugging herself pretty heavy for a woman who didn't usually drink much, but it didn't change the way she looked. She could live on gin and downers at Mom Jenny's until she died. Then the guys at the morgue would wonder how such a ladylike stiff ever managed to make such a mess of herself.

Essie gulped down the last of her drink and got unsteadily to her feet. Shad, leaving his Scotch only half finished, handed the bartender a five-dollar bill and said with aplomb, "Keep the change," and strolled out of the lounge two minutes after Essie. She was easy to spot in the uncrowded waiting room, slim and staggering a little on her bird-thin legs and high-heeled shoes as she walked toward Gate 6. Shad followed close behind her, not caring whether she noticed him. But with two double vodka martinis and two downers under her belt, she wasn't noticing much.

He took the seat behind her on the plane and heard her tell the stewardess, who had practically guided Essie to her seat, "I'll be asleep before we even take off—two sleeping pills—so will you please wake me up and see that I get off the plane in Louisville."

As the stewardess looked down at Essie, her look seemed to say, "And too much liquor to boot," and her suspicions were verified by Shad, who put his thumb to his mouth and threw back his head as a signal.

"My mother's in danger ... maybe murder," jabbered Essie, slurring her words. "Nobody knows I'm coming. I didn't tell Star—Star's my daughter—I'm coming. Jus' made a dash for the plane. I'll spend the night at the Brown Hotel an' take a taxi out in the morning." Essie babbled on. "The sound of a car goin' up that hill an' honkin' in the middle of the night would scare hell outta 'em all. . . . "

"Yes, ma'am," the stewardess agreed. She had learned long ago not to argue with drunken passengers.

Shad agreed too, silently. His plans included a visit to Tom's wilderness tonight, and he much preferred being the only late visitor—a noiseless one, at that.

A woman sitting by the window next to Essie gathered her belongings and clambered over Essie, who had passed out completely while the stewardess was still staring at her, and took the seat beside Shad.

Shad had to smile over the move: it pays to be careful who you get close to these days. The woman was happy to have pointedly put some distance between herself and a distasteful drunk, only she didn't know she'd jumped from the skillet into the fire. It was going to be easy and not too risky, just before he left the plane, to lift her wallet from that purse.

When the plane landed in Louisville, Essie had to be

awakened, and on leaving the plane, she practically sleep-walked to the baggage area, weaving this way and that.

Estelle must be very sick, Shad thought, because he knew Essie wasn't a lush. She'd knocked herself out to get away from feeling. Maybe the feeling Estelle would die. That remark about murder might mean she was on to something. Or *in* on something. There's nothing like liquor to bring out what's eating at a person. Well, he didn't see any way her plans could interfere with his.

Shad walked from the Louisville airport to a gas station on Preston Street with his usual slouch and swagger, cigarette hanging from his lower lip as if stuck to it. Then just before entering the radius of light that encircled the gas station, he changed his entire demeanor. First, he flipped the cigarette into the blackened snow of the gutter. Then he composed his features into a choirboy expression and walked into the gas station, using the Dr. Snyder stroll again.

Within minutes after entering the station, he'd struck up an amiable and, on his part, deferential conversation with a truck driver who was only too glad to give such a nice, well-mannered kid a lift out Highway 42.

It was great zooming up and down the hills of Kentucky in the biggest thing on wheels. If he could only be the driver! And he could if he wanted to enough. There were ways. But Tom's car would be better—easier to get and to disguise. And plenty big enough to hold more than Shad planned to take from the Morgan home—all the cash he could find and six gold teaspoons that had belonged to Tom's mother. And maybe some silver, and one or two small pieces of jewelry. If he could get into Estelle's room. And the TV, of course.

"What'd ya say yer folks' name was?" the truck driver asked, once under way.

"Morgan. Tom Morgan's a real big name around here."

"Yeah?"

"Well, I'm telling ya. And he's rich, owns newspapers, land—you name it."

"Yer kidding," the driver said.

"Nope. And with money like that behind me, I can do what I want. I could get away with murder and the cops couldn't prove a thing—or wouldn't try."

"Why mess up your life, kid?" the driver said. "Where'd ya say you wanted me to drop you?"

"Up the road a ways—I'll let you know in plenty of time," Shad answered. Then, frustrated by feeling he hadn't sufficiently impressed the driver, he pulled out his switchblade, snapped it open, and toyed with it. A glance at the driver's face revealed to Shad that he had now succeeded.

The truck had reached the top of a long hill, and the headlights shone down a steep blacktop slope and spread a soft glow along the wooded edges of a lonely valley.

"I'll get out at the foot of this hill," Shad said, and laughed. He was proud of his scare tactics.

When the driver stopped the truck, Shad jumped out.

"So long, kid," the driver said. "If you ask me, you're looking for trouble."

Shad laughed again—he'd really scared the man. That C. Clyde voice scared everybody, everybody except the old lady, Estelle.

Shad climbed the fence to the right of the road and walked several yards into the woods along the bank of a broad creek. It was cold, blood-freezing cold. The snow came over his shoe tops. His bones all but clacked out loud. He'd be lucky if his toes didn't freeze off before he made it to the Morgan house. In this kind of cold, if you stopped to rest, you'd get sleepy and never wake up.

He rounded a bend in the creek and his flashlight, probing among the trees and brush ahead, glittered on the ice of a smaller creek, one small enough to step across, flowing into the big one. It was a nice-sized creek for coons to easily catch fish or anything else that might wander down for a drink—a good spot for poachers who now and then got around the Morgan defenses.

Shad paused; the scene reminded him of an incident that happened two or three years ago. He was spending the Christmas holidays with the Morgans, and Estelle had taken him on a walk through the wilderness to show him animal tracks in the snow and point out some of the creek scenery she was so stuck on. He smiled as he remembered that hike, because Estelle ended up breaking the law. They had found a coon caught in a trap and Shad freed it. Estelle took the trap home, which was stealing. She said so herself. She was embarrassed by what she did, though, and tried to pass it off by explaining that even though the trap was illegally set on someone else's land, it really belonged to the trapper—but that in this case it was like breaking the fugitive-slave laws of long ago: it was the lesser of two evils.

The whole thing was crazy, Shad thought. Do-gooders never achieve anything. He was sure of that—he himself was living proof of it. That's what the judge said after going through all those papers about the psychiatric treatment Estelle had provided. He said it with a sad look, but he'd said it.

But it was too shivering cold to stand there remembering. He stepped across the small creek and walked up it a way. Suddenly something ahead gleamed in the light from his flash. Eyes. The eyes of a trapped coon. Just like the one he'd helped Estelle rescue near this very spot.

The coon tried to pull free but its delicate black fingers were caught tight. Shad fished in his pocket for the strong piece of cord he always carried and quickly made a noose. The coon snarled when Shad attempted to drop the noose over its head and missed. He was so damned cold he could hardly operate. He leaned closer, hoping the fool animal wouldn't bite him. This time he got the noose over its head and jerked it tight. In a couple of seconds the coon was unconscious, maybe dead. Shad opened the trap and released the inert animal. He touched its side and felt a heartbeat. Then he carefully felt the paw that had been caught in the steel jaws; it was not damaged—still warm and no bones broken. He loosened the noose, muttering, "You'll be all right, old man, as soon as you get your breath again."

By the time he got the trap unfastened from the tree root that held it, the coon had come to and tottered to its feet. It looked at Shad, kind of dopey. He liked animals, especially wild ones—the wilder the better. The kind that can't be taught any law. Any more than he could.

Shad carried the trap with him until he came to a dense thicket, where he flung it away. Not that getting rid of it would help a single solitary animal but it would sure make a church-goin' poacher mad as hell. A pleasant thought.

He worked his way up the hill through the woods, keeping clear of the road, and approached the Morgan house by way of the grape arbor. A good place, not easily seen. He

102

remembered it was here Star had tried to open the escape hatch for sinners. He enjoyed the thought that Star would never be able to dig *his* grandmother out of hell—it was his grandmother who told him often enough that he was the devil's bastard, and after a time, a long time, he got to like the idea. Having the devil himself for a father might turn out useful in his line of work: crime.

He laughed to himself and thought of his grandmother. "Fry the old bat good, Dad," he said. "Keep her roasting, rare to well-done, around the clock."

When he reached the house, he carefully scouted around to be sure no one else was wandering about, then slipped up the ladder leading to Estelle's window. At the top, he cautiously peered in. At first he saw only the back of some woman. She turned her head and he recognized Ginelda, with her ear close to Estelle's mouth, listening intently. They were right, Estelle must be real sick—and evidently scared, too, the way she was clinging to Ginelda's arm. From the look on the old lady's face, whatever she had to whisper was important as hell; it was the same kind of look she used to give him when she tried to impress on him the sins of stealing. But this time it was like her life depended on what she was saying, not his—or Ginelda's. He wished he could hear what it was about, but he couldn't. The way Ginelda had to lean so close to hear, Estelle's voice must be mighty weak.

There was no sense in watching this scene any longer, Shad thought, and silently climbed down the ladder and went to the one leading to the back bedroom. He could see that Star was the only one in that room, asleep in her clothes, with all the lights on. What a dish! But where was

103

Tom? Had he put Star in this room and moved to the cabin?

Then he decided he'd better case the downstairs. But before he was all the way down the ladder he saw a light in the distance, slowly coming up the hill, coming right up the road. What the hell . . . ? He couldn't stand there on the ladder waiting to find out, so he jumped to the ground and slipped into the open garage to wait.

It was too dark to make things out clearly, but from what he could see, Shad knew the visitor was a man and that he carried a flashlight. He gradually came closer, and slanted the light toward the ground, turned it toward the garage. But evidently he wasn't looking for cars, for he passed by not far from where Shad stood, out of sight. From the cut of his clothes and the type of suitcase, Shad decided it was some young square who didn't want to be seen and by the looks of things, one who didn't know his way around. He passed by the Morgan house without examining it, but did stop to examine the big chicken house in the back yard. Stopped and stared at it thoughtfully, as if wondering about it.

A chicken thief dressed like that? No. What, then? Elementary, dear Watson. Just a guy who doesn't know where the hell he is. But Morgan's wilderness is a funny place to end up lost at this time of night. And with a suitcase.

The visitor looked around some more and then turned toward what he must have been looking for in the first place—the cabin. For he walked right in the door, like he knew it would be unlocked. Like a guest. What school did Estelle send him to? Shad wondered.

In order to get a better idea of what was happening, Shad crept to a window at the rear of the cabin, where he felt it was safe to peer in and study the man. No lights were turned on, and the stranger placed his suitcase at the foot of the bed and then removed his overcoat and jacket. Next he explored the room and bathroom, keeping his flashlight always pointed toward the floor—not like a guest at all. This was a man who didn't want to be seen. Then he returned to the bed, sat and took off his shoes, and stuck the flashlight in one of them—a good system for knowing just where it is, Shad realized, with a touch of respect—and lay on one of the twin beds, pulling a blanket over himself.

While wondering what step to take next, Shad saw the man throw off the blanket, get up and walk to a front window facing the big house. He stood a while as if studying the house, but Shad figured all he could see was the outline of the building, which had a couple of lighted rooms. After his long look, he returned to the bed, but he was nervous about something, for he lay only a few minutes before rising again and going to the window to look toward the big house. Then back to bed, only to repeat his maneuver a few more times. Finally, he lay still a spell, long enough for Shad to feel like he was going to freeze waiting for the jerk to calm down. Then Shad sneaked to the front door and very quietly, expertly, opened it: the man was not only asleep now but snoring softly. Dead to the world. Shad entered the cabin, wishing someone could be here to witness how well he was pulling off this cat-job. He was a mere shadow gliding among thoroughly familiar shapes. He'd slept here many a vacation night. He stood absolutely still, waiting to see if the man heard him. It was not a long wait; a rhythm in the snoring had developed by now.

Who was this dude? Was he a square? Maybe not. Rich guys do take a flyer at crime now and then. Usually without

105

making out too well. It took years of training—like his, Shad's—to be this good, he proudly told himself. He went to the dresser where the guy had put his wallet, watch, change and a pack of cigarettes, nearly full. He scooped up the loot and hastily made his exit. Outside the cabin, he squatted to surreptitiously examine the wallet by flashlight: a hundred and ten dollars in tens and twenties, plus a good watch, maybe real gold. Neat work, Shad, he congratulated himself. While still crouched, he ducked his head, cupped his hands and lit one of the newly acquired cigarettes. Now to re-examine the big house and make an even bigger haul. . . .

Shad went first to the sun porch, hoping and fully expecting it would be empty. Looking for a possible point of entry, he moved up to the window that faced the back yard and raised his head to peer in. A faint light shone into the sun porch through the half-open door between it and the kitchen.

Shad almost fell back into the dark at the sight of the hospital bed and Tom. For a moment he had an alarmed conviction that Tom had seen him, or at least the glow of the cigarette. He snuffed out the cigarette by thrusting its tip into the snow, put the butt in his pocket, and cautiously approached the window again.

Tom had not stirred. He looked as near dead as Estelle. His eyes were closed. Had they been closed when Shad first looked in? He wasn't sure. He was struck by a sense of uneasiness and the half thrill of a close call. But he better not stand around thinking about it. If Tom wasn't already dead, it would kill him sure to wake in the morning and see his lawn decorated with an ice statue of his favorite foster son, Shad.

He decided to enter the house by climbing through
Ginelda's bathroom window. He made sure it was empty and
was thankful he had gloves on—a touch he didn't forget. He
was familiar with Ginelda's quarters: the small bath, her
bedroom across from it, separated by a short and narrow
entrance hall from the kitchen. Her bedroom door was open,
so a quick glance told him both hallway and bedroom were
empty. The door leading to the kitchen was slightly ajar but
he didn't dare close it, though Ginelda must still be upstairs
taking care of Estelle. What a break!

He was cold, he realized, and tired, and he had to think
and plan. What better place than under Ginelda's bed! He
slid under the dust ruffles, which touched the floor, screening
him from any prying eyes, and stretched out on the lux-
urious, deep-pile carpet—bought especially for Ginelda to
ease the rheumatism in her feet. In fact, he'd noticed the
whole room was as he remembered it—a look and feel of
comfort, though sparsely furnished—a single bed, with a
dresser on the entrance side and night table on the other,
with its own telephone. Ginelda insisted on her privacy. A
rocker, two straight chairs and a highboy were the only other
furnishings. An old-fashioned room, and he'd never felt so
warm and comfortable, safe and rich. And so proud of a
night's work. Or more full of plans for a profitable tomorrow.

CHAPTER X

SHAD HAD NOT meant to fall asleep and risk getting caught. But he had, and was now awakened by the cackling of female voices in the kitchen. The smell of fresh coffee almost made him join them. A quick glance at George's watch told him it was 7:30—he had been asleep for hours!

Then a door opened and there was a sudden silence, finally broken by Ginelda's voice—he'd know that voice anywhere. "Well, Miz Purdie, time you got here. I been all night with your patient.... "

"Is she all right?" interrupted the voice called Miz Purdie. "And where's Star?"

"Calm yourself, Miz Purdie. Ain't like you to be upset. And don't worry—she was sometimes real clear and then she'd fade clean away. But now both ladies is asleep, her and Star. Star had a splittin' headache and took somethin' for it and fell asleep in that room where you put them medicines. I jus' let her sleep. A good thing I did, too, if you ask me. Here's your coffee, Miz Purdie."

"Not till I've seen my patient," was the reply, and a hasty tread died away.

"Didn't even have time to tell her about Miz Morgan's gettin' up outta bed," said Ginelda. "She'd sure have a fit if she knew about *that.*"

"If she slept in like the rest of us, we wouldn't have all this fuss," said a voice.

"But she's got a husband," said Ginelda, not too kindly. "More coffee, Trudy? Here you are—an' put some bread in that toaster," she added. "Miz Purdie'll be back in a jiffy and be askin' for it. Always wants things on the dot, that one."

The chatter continued, and after a while Shad heard someone enter the kitchen. "Well, she's sleeping, all right. And like a log, I might say. So I'll take my coffee here—right now, she wouldn't know if I was there or not. Where's my toast?"

Then Shad heard a volley of voices. "Oh, Mr. Harry—and Miz Morgan!" cried Ginelda. "You're here early."

A fusillade of words greeted the newcomers. Sounded like a convention. Several women competing to impress Harry and Katinka with sensational news. Shad could make no sense out of the babble until one of the ladies said, "Your mother walked right down all them steps. Alone!"

"Oh, my God, no . . . " moaned Harry.

"What did you say?" demanded the Purdie voice.

"Just flew all the way down and out here to Mr. Morgan!"

"Where the hell were all of you?" asked Harry.

Apparently no one heard him. "And us thinking she was so weak!"

"Just flew," someone insisted, "or floated, quiet as a ghost, and just as fast, or else I'd have seen her, because I was with Mr. Morgan all night, except a minute's coffee break while I slipped in Ginelda's room to put my hair in these curlers. . . ."

Shad never heard so many trying to talk at the same time, each telling the same story according to her own version. He tried to figure out how many people were in there. Ginelda and Harry and Katinka; the one called Miz Purdie, who must be Estelle's nurse; Trudy, who was Tom's night nurse, and two more voices—they must be nurses also. Seven people—he thought, My God, I'll never get out of here with that mob next door!

"We was all in Ginelda's room—the three of us. Remember? Just talking and fixin' our hair. Ginelda lets us use her room for things like that. That's why none of us seen her come through the kitchen on her way to Mr. Morgan."

All of this must have happened way before his arrival, Shad thought. Certainly all was quiet and dark when he first cased the house. He had to smile—there was probably precious little these nurses didn't hear or see. Yet, he thought, here in this little room they wouldn't have been able to hear a herd of buffalo during their gabfests and haircurling session. None of them. And with Ginelda upstairs all that time—only she *was* hearing something. Something secret from Estelle. He wondered what *that* was all about.

"If you could have seen her!" said one. "Or could have heard Miss Star screaming. Made my blood run cold. It all happened because Miss Star fell asleep on the job, if you ask me."

"Mrs. Morgan needs a professional nurse at night. Not a kid."

"Miss Star does her best," said Ginelda. "But somebody ought to have an eye on Miz Morgan every minute. A *responsible* eye," said Ginelda, "especially after what she told me ... "

Practically in unison they all asked, "What?"

"Yes, Ginelda, what did she tell you?" asked Harry.

"Nothin' important," said Ginelda, in a hedging tone now. "Jus' asked me to call Mr. Ashton this morning. I'll tell you about it later, Mr. Harry. Right now I'm goin' to finish my cocoa and then I'll make my call and then get me some sleep. I was up all night. I don't want nobody comin' in my room till I get up, not even openin' my door."

"She's right," said Harry. "Let her rest as long as she wants. And you, Mrs. Purdie, get on upstairs to my mother—that's where you should be right now. And you," he added in his foreman tone, "get to my father—he's there all by himself!"

Shad heard the two nurses scurry off, and then Katinka said, "I'll meet you upstairs, Harry. I'm going to the front hall and call home and check on the children." Shad heard her leave the kitchen.

"And I've got to go unload that chicken feed from my car out back—four big sacks." Harry sighed. "Well, get lots of sleep, Ginelda."

Now Shad wondered who was left in the kitchen. And he found out when one of the nurses said, "Well, everybody's skedaddled—just us three left. Now we can have our coffee in peace."

"Not me," said the one called Trudy. "I been up all night with Mr. Morgan. I'm off to get my shut-eye."

"Well, I might as well head for the laundry room and press a couple of my uniforms," said the other. "Sleep well, Ginelda."

"I will," said Ginelda, "just as soon as I finish this cocoa. Makes me sleep better."

That leaves only Ginelda, Shad thought, lying quietly under the bed. Maybe I can get out of here before she finishes her cocoa.

But at that moment he heard her enter the small hallway leading to her bedroom. After all the noise of only a few minutes ago, the room seemed like a tomb. He could tell from the movement on the deep carpet that Ginelda was in the room and had come around to the far side of the bed, next to the telephone, and sat down. The mattress sank toward him.

And then he heard the dialing of the phone. It delighted him to think of the terror his presence would cause if Ginelda became aware of him under the bed. The dialing stopped and Shad heard a busy signal. Ginelda hung up, waited only a minute and dialed again. Still busy. Another pause and she began to dial again.

And as she did, Shad became conscious of a depression of the carpet pile on the other side of the bed. Someone else was in the room and had not made a sound. There was only a dust ruffle between him and the other person's feet. Suddenly Shad heard a heavy clunk. Something hard and heavy hitting something not so hard. And then something fell, landing on the carpet near his head, just beyond the bed's skirt, where the night table would be. And with that a second object fell, only it fell heavily across the bed, landing with a great pressure on the mattress and springs. And then nothing but silence in the room, except for a faint buzz which told Shad that the phone lay on the floor. He could see the carpet depress as the intruder walked around the bed, picked up the phone, put the receiver in its cradle and placed it on the night table. He heard the person leave the room, heard the door close. Silence again. He waited for what seemed an eternity, probably five minutes, and cautiously lifted the skirt on the door side of the bed and saw nothing to arouse his suspicions. He wriggled his way from under the bed, and then he saw her—Ginelda. Lying backward across the bed, the top of her head bashed in. There was an iron beside her, all messed up, smeared with blood and grayish lumps of crushed brains—and an ever-widening red stain on the counterpane. It took muscle to do that, Shad breathed in revulsion—a man. And then it hit him—the guy in the cabin.

But why would he kill Ginelda? And if he didn't, then who did—one of that kitchen claque?

No matter who or why—Ginelda was dead and he'd be the one to hang for it if he didn't get the hell out of there. Fast. He staggered into the tiny bathroom. Its window gave a view of the turnaround, where there were three cars: a Cadillac he hadn't seen before, Katinka's same old sedan, and Harry's convertible. That's funny—why the separate cars? Oh yeah, Harry had to use his to haul that feed.

Between him and the cars was a clean sheet of unmarked snow. Much of it had fallen in the night, after he got in the house, covering his tracks. Now it was ready to record every step he made in getting out of here, a record as easy to read as a goddamned newspaper.

Knowing Harry, his keys would be in the ignition of the convertible, but a convertible was designed to be the worst getaway car in the whole U.S.A. Katinka's sedan? Knowing Katinka, the keys were safely in her purse. The Cadillac? No way of telling about those keys. Besides, if he made a dash for it, he might run into somebody. Wasn't Harry out there somewhere with his chicken feed? And any attempt to reach the garage and back Tom's car out would be reckless. No matter how he figured it, there would only be him and his tracks. . . .

No, he couldn't try that now. Too risky. He'd hang for it. He could feel himself swinging by the neck, eyes popped, tongue thickened, his head whirling. Then he heard someone in the kitchen—he dashed back into Ginelda's room, tried not to look at her body, and ducked under the bed again, to be covered while he thought out a plan. A plan that wouldn't leave tracks on the gleaming new snow.

He was cold in the warm room; a stream of sweat crawled like a snake down his back. He tried to stiffen his body against the shaking that possessed him like palsy. He must forget what lay on the mattress above him and think. When it—her body—was found, there'd be a thorough search of the house. He'd be done for, unless he'd figured out how to escape first. There must be a way if he could think of it in time.

115

He had to listen, think, keep his eyes open. He listened so hard it was as if his whole body were one great ear. But all he could hear was silence. His body began to shake harder, as though he had malaria.

CHAPTER XI

WHILE UNLOADING THE chicken feed, it dawned on Harry that he should have gone up to see his mother before doing anything else, just as soon as he heard about her getting up out of bed and coming downstairs. But if she was asleep, as Mrs. Purdie and Ginelda assured him she was, what good would it have done him to go up? What got him was that none of the nurses, nor Ginelda, had actually seen Estelle come down the stairs, but just hearing about it made Harry feel he had. Had seen and heard a bone-cracking fall—and yet, she had not fallen. She had somehow got safely to Tom. Through the maze of Medici fantasies and the halls, stairs, and rooms of a big house, she'd had the strength and sense to get to Tom. Her natural protector.

He reentered the house, crossed into the dining room, and heard quick, rubber-soled steps upstairs. When he reached the front hall, he saw Katinka still issuing instructions over the phone to the day worker. Mrs. Purdie was at the head of the stairs.

"Don't bother to come down," he called to her, but she descended, a finger on her lips. They met at the foot of the stairs, she standing one step up looking down at him, smoothing her skirt with her large, be-ringed fingers spread wide.

"I'm going to have a little visit with Mother," he said.

"Oh, Mr. Morgan, I wouldn't advise you to go up just now. She's sleeping so well, she really shouldn't be disturbed."

"Has she been awake at all since you came on duty?"

"Not for a minute."

"Then maybe it would be good to wake her now, give her some breakfast. . . . "

"Oh, I feel strongly it wouldn't. After such exertion—I don't think she should be disturbed yet. Sleep is the greatest healer."

The stairs were steep and narrow. Mrs. Purdie, tall, something of a beauty, Amazon style, barred the way completely. This physical fact, plus his respect for her undeniable right to exercise sickroom authority, made him hesitate.

Then he said, with a burst of irritation, "Maybe it would be best not to wake her, but I intend to at least have a quick look at her." He had a fleeting impression that Mrs. Purdie was about to bar his way by force, but he started up the stairs, and at the last possible moment, she stood aside and let him pass.

An uneasy feeling suddenly overwhelmed Harry. His mother had always been a light sleeper, but now he made no

effort to keep down the noise his heavy boots made on the
uncarpeted stairs. One of his more unpleasant memories of
childhood had to do with being required to tiptoe or whisper
through part of the day when she was trying to sleep because
of a headache or to get rested for an evening party. Odd that
she'd been undisturbed by his honking at the curves coming
up the hill—or the conversation with Mrs. Purdie just below
her room. Mrs. Purdie had whispered but he had spoken in a
normal voice. And now his resounding footsteps . . .

He charged up the remaining stairs and along the hall to
the door of his mother's room. He opened it and rushed in,
Mrs. Purdie following.

"Mr. Morgan!" she gasped, her tone and expression full of
shocked reproof.

His mother lay absolutely still, eyes closed, face peaceful.
"Mother!" he cried with sudden foreboding at the pit of his
stomach.

There was no reaction except a martyred sigh from Mrs.
Purdie calling Heaven's attention to the fact that she'd done
all *she* could to protect her patient from this brutal intrusion.

Harry spoke louder, even sharply. "Mother!" Then he
leaned over and put his hand on her left shoulder, pressing a
little and calling again, "Mother!"

She opened her mouth but not her eyes, and uttered a low
guttural sound that made Harry's insides quiver with horror.
He shook her.

Mrs. Purdie, beginning to look as agitated as he, almost
shouted, "Mrs. Morgan, wake up!"

Harry thrust his arm under his mother's bony shoulders
and raised her slightly. Her head sagged like a broken doll's.
She made another sound, a meaningless rumble in the throat,

119

eyes still closed. He laid her back on the pillows and stared at Mrs. Purdie. "She's dying!"

"Oh no, Mr. Morgan, don't say that! We're just sleeping very soundly—I'm sure that's all it is."

"Call Dr. Clifford. Tell my wife to come up—and call my sister. You have her New York number?"

"Yes. Yes. I'll call them all and be back in a jiffy. I'm sure everything will be all right."

"Don't wake Star. She's too young for this."

"Yes, sir," she said.

It was only after Purdie left the room that the full impact of what was happening really hit him. Hit him with stunning force. She was dying as he watched. Drawing her last few breaths in the same bed in which he'd drawn his first. He bent double, wedging his body against his arms to lock in the sorrow that was draining him like a hidden wound. He mustn't let go now, lose control of himself. Out of her bones she had borne him and now—now he must take this parting. Take it with all his strength. He must ignore the suddenly terrified child in himself that wanted to cry out, "Don't leave me."

But the cry, the feeling of a cry not quite heard, wouldn't choke down. It was as if it were not even inside him, but in her. An appeal from her weakness to his strength, pulling at him. Like that long-ago morning when she woke him at dawn, looking pale, frightened, wanting him to be the one to drive her to the hospital because Tom was away in Washington. At that time, she wasn't Mother anymore, but simply a girl with long brown hair who needed him, a man, to take care of her. A few hours later, when he heard that her

120

longed-for third child had been stillborn, some lines of poetry floated through his mind, "Don't cry, little girl, don't cry,/ They've broken your doll, I know," and he was unable to keep from crying himself, in front of Dr. Clifford and the obstetrician.

"Maybe it's for the best," one of them said. "It can be hard on a woman to start all over with a new baby at forty. Forty is old for that."

He needed Katinka. What was keeping her? And Mrs. Purdie? Oh, what a worm he was—wanting them, wanting not to be alone with his grief. With her. And with the knowledge, now felt in a new way, that he would die, too, someday, and Katinka and his soft-skinned baby daughters.

"Dr. Clifford should be here any minute," Mrs. Purdie told Harry and Katinka. "His receptionist said he'd called in and told her he would come out here instead of going to the office. And that your sister will be with him."

"Essie? She couldn't be—not yet—I mean, Dr. Clifford wouldn't have called her if he hadn't foreseen this!"

"She called *him*, from the Brown Hotel. Flew down last night on impulse, the receptionist said. So he's giving her a ride out here. Coincidence. It has to be coincidence."

Or had Essie had an intuition. . . . She'd never been gifted with much feminine intuition, but still. . . .

Mrs. Purdie took Estelle's pulse. "We're better," she whispered, "I do think we're better."

Harry's heart quickened with unexpected hope. She had whispered. People whisper when they feel the sick may hear.

Then, hearing something outside, he stepped quickly to

the window. A car was coming to a stop on the turnaround. Dr. Clifford got out and opened the door for Essie. "They're here! Go let them in!" he cried to Mrs. Purdie.

Essie entered the room first, with Dr. Clifford close on her heels. She glanced a wordless greeting to Harry and then stared at her mother with a look of shock and growing anger.

Dr. Clifford's examination was brief, even cursory, it seemed to Harry. Estelle muttered a little at the cold pressure of the stethoscope, but she didn't open her eyes.

"Has she a chance, any chance?" Harry asked.

"She'll be all right. Her vital signs are good," Dr. Clifford said. "Don't worry."

Essie looked around and asked, "Where's Star?"

"She's in the back room," said Harry, "still asleep—she wasn't well last night."

"I'll go wake her," said Essie.

Essie put her hand on her daughter's shoulder and said softly, "Star."

Star's wide eyes opened and met her mother's with amazement, followed almost instantly by delight. Then she did something—quite unaware of what she did—that made Essie ache for a time long past.

Star held out both arms to her mother in exactly the same way, and even with the same expression, she had as an infant, when Essie leaned over the cradle and said, "Take, take," meaning I want to take you up in my arms.

Star was no longer of a size to be picked up, but Essie sat down and enfolded her in a joyful embrace. Joy with pain in it. They might never have such a moment again. Holding her, even rocking her just a little, she told her everything she'd learned from Dr. Clifford on the ride out—all his suspicions that somebody'd been drugging or poisoning Estelle.

"And I had to fall asleep—oh, Essie, I feel so guilty."

"Don't, Star. Ginelda was with her."

"But there's a murderer after all!" Star cried.

"I'm afraid so, dear. But we'll see to it there's no murder."

"But who's been doing it?" Star asked. "And how?"

"We'll find out," Essie said. "Meanwhile, Estelle must be guarded every minute."

"Yes, we can take turns," Star said. "And this time I won't fall asleep on my tour."

"I had a good night's sleep on the plane, and later at the Brown Hotel," Essie said, without mentioning the unaccustomed drinks and pills. "So you can have a partly free day, now that I'm here. Get some more sleep down in the cabin. But not all day. You're going to prepare all Estelle's meals from now on. Don't let anyone else touch a pot, dish or the tray. Dr. Clifford's with Estelle now ... "

At that moment, Essie was interrupted by the explosive entrance of George. "Star! The nurse said you were in here."

"George!" cried Essie.

"Oh, George!" cried Star, rushing to his arms.

"Uh, Essie ... hello." And then he turned to Star. "I've been robbed—all my money, my watch, even my cigarettes!"

"Robbed? A murderer and now a thief!"

"Who's a murderer?" asked George.

"We don't know," replied Essie. "Star, what *is* going on?"

"I meant to tell you, Essie. George arrived last night and slept in the cabin. He's going to be there with me a few days."

123

Essie had been a professional actress for several years of her girlhood. The sexual revolution had actually occurred in the theater a few decades before anything in her memory, even before the birth of the State of Kentucky, or even Bard College—St. Stephens it was called then. Her participation had only lasted for three weeks, at twenty-three, and she had never felt less like discussing it than now.

"Oh, for God's sakes, Star! Do you really think this is the time for such behavior?"

"I called him last night because I was scared and wanted him here to protect me and Estelle. And maybe we'll all need him."

George, six feet tall, very sinewy. Only a few pimples left over from a once severe case of adolescent acne. He saw the dismay in Essie's eyes and read the reaction in Star's face. "Don't worry, Essie," he said, "there are twin beds in the cabin."

"Great! Next best thing to a chastity belt," Essie said ironically. "Star, at least hold out until I can get you the pill."

"Only very immature girls leave *that* to their mothers," Star said. "I got a prescription two days after I met George, and have been taking it faithfully ever since, just in case, but I'm still a virgin. Meanwhile, considering that Estelle is in real danger, you should be glad to have a man around. A poisoner or a thief who gets frustrated, or even flustered, could start slugging or something," she went on. "In that case, you can phone the cabin for George."

"I will," said Essie weakly, "but in the meantime we better get George back to that cabin before Tom finds out

he's staying there with you. It would be the death of him. . . .
Oh, my, I wish I hadn't said that!"

In spite of her own past—Essie and Mark had felt
gloriously liberated being lovers for three weeks before she
dramatically gave up her career to marry him—she wasn't at
all happy to see Star standing "where brook and river meet"
with such very unreluctant feet.

After George had gone and while Star was brushing her
hair, Essie said, "Now be sure and keep him out of Tom's
sight."

"Never fear, I wouldn't expect *Tom* to understand," Star
said. "I haven't discussed George with anyone down here
except Estelle, when she was less confused than recently."

Essie groaned audibly. "Well, I'm going back to stay with
her now." She'd thought watching her unconscious mother
would be the worst part of the day. But Star had managed to
top even that.

This girl-child of hers would, she knew, brush her hair to a
lustrous sheen, and brush it again, and preen before present-
ing herself to a boy who—unless he, too, was really in love—
would clasp the nearest available female like a frog.

But he had flown down here, though New York was full of
girls. That proved he was more discriminating than a frog.

Still, she wished he'd flown to the North Pole instead.

"Has she had any episodes like this before, Mrs. Purdie?"
Dr. Clifford asked, as Essie reentered the room.

"I don't know, sir. I don't think so. If I'd thought so, I'd
have reported it. She's slept a good deal every day, but I
don't know if—if it was ever *more* than sleep before this. Be-

because I never tried to wake her before. On the contrary, I felt she needed all the rest she could get."

"Quite right," Dr. Clifford said.

Dr. Clifford was already setting up some kind of equipment by the bedside. "Well, it struck me early this morning that intravenous feeding was called for, and I decided to make it my first order of business for today. I'm certainly glad now that I did. It'll bring her around."

"But wouldn't a hospital . . . "

"No, with Mrs. Purdie and Essie to help me, we can manage here."

"Mother's gown doesn't look as if it has been changed since I left two weeks ago," Essie said to Mrs. Purdie.

"I wanted to change it yesterday, but we didn't want anyone to move our poor arm and I—I . . . " Mrs. Purdie's tone was righteousness offended— "I didn't insist."

"I'll cut it off her," Essie said, "without moving her arm at all." No one ever moved that arm except when Estelle had taken a strong pain killer. Estelle herself, when well, soaked it long enough in the tub in hot water for cleanliness, without unbending it. "Where are the scissors?" Essie asked.

"Here," Katinka said, handing her a pair.

"Mrs. Purdie, you can get everything ready for her bath. Basin, warm water, soap, wash cloth. . . . "

"I know what's needed," Mrs. Purdie sniffed. "When Dr. Clifford can spare me."

"And I'll slit one of her other gowns down the front, like a hospital gown, so it can be put on easily," Katinka said, getting one out of the bureau drawer. Faded pink. "Later today, I'll buy her half a dozen new ones, all open-down-the-front types."

126

"Good idea," Essie said, speaking in a pleasant tone for the first time. Mrs. Purdie, still helping Dr. Clifford arrange the bottle and tubes, looked more injured than ever. Blamed for what she couldn't help.

"Let's go home, Harry," Katinka said. "Even unconscious, Estelle still wouldn't want you to see her bathed."

"I can wait in the living room."

"We're going home," Katinka said. "Naomi seems to be coming down with something. I want you to have a look at her."

"She was blooming a couple of hours ago!"

"You know how quickly they can droop at her age. *Please* come."

"Well. . . . " Harry was more puzzled than alarmed. "I won't leave the house once I get there," he said. "Call me whenever you have the slightest reason, Mrs. Purdie."

"Yes, sir, I certainly will."

He hoped addressing this last remark to Mrs. Purdie would soothe her feelings, so obviously ruffled by Essie's abruptness.

"I won't leave until I'm sure everything is under control," Dr. Clifford promised. "Then I'll give you a ring myself. Or, on second thought, I'll drop by. I can take a look at Naomi and tell you whether you need to call a pediatrician."

"Do that, please," Katinka said. "Come on, Harry. Let's go in my car. Leave yours for Essie or Star in case they need it."

CHAPTER XII

Shad again looked at George's watch. He'd been lying there at least a couple of hours! If he could get to the bathroom for a minute, or have a cup of that coffee he kept smelling—anything to relieve his present situation. How did he get into this, anyway—he who prided himself on smooth, silent and non-violent pursuit of crime? Real loot within his grasp, his career just budding—and maybe about to be terminated. He couldn't get out and wait around in the room, not with Ginelda and her brains lying on the bed. Why in hell didn't somebody come and find her body? Then he remembered her warning to them all not to disturb her, no matter what the reason. God—he could be here hours yet before anyone came in.

During the two hours he had already been under the bed, he had heard one car drive up. Who was the new arrival, or arrivals? Then later a car drove off down the hill. So three cars were still there. Three cars left, and he had to get away in one of them.

And there still was a very silent and efficient murderer wandering around somewhere out there. If that one ever found out Shad had been under the bed when the murder took place, then his death would be quicker than by hanging. Still, he wished he'd seen who the killer was, had really been a witness. Course nobody would believe him. Whenever it had been his word against someone else's, that someone else had it made.

Then he heard a voice. Not in the kitchen—a voice nearer and very clear. Tom's! Tom, near enough to touch if one very thin partition between the rooms—and beds—were removed. By lying still and concentrating, he could make out the words.

"What I need is to get on my feet," Tom said. "Up and around. I should have managed by now. A bump on the head shouldn't flatten a man for six weeks."

Then Shad heard Star's voice: "You've had a stroke," she reminded Tom gently.

"Stroke-shmoke, as my old friend Judge Solomon Bloom would have said. Pure nonsense. Something struck me on the head."

Tom was the kind of kook who *would* have judges for friends. And Shad had known that particular judge too, in Juvenile Court. He had dropped dead a couple of years later from a stroke, according to the newspaper account a pal sent Shad.

Suddenly a startling racket, a mixture of heavy objects thrashing about and bedsprings complaining loudly, assaulted Shad's ears.

"Tom! Don't!" Star's voice was louder.

The unholy noise ceased as suddenly as it had begun.

"Sit down, Star, and lower your voice," Tom said in his prison-guard tone. "I don't want those cackling geese—excuse me, I mean those worthy, dedicated nurses, to come clucking in here. I won't have my exercises interfered with."

Exercises? Shad wondered. Was that how he made the racket?

"Do you think you should be sitting up like that with your back unsupported?" Star asked.

"Yes, I've been doing it every day since I regained consciousness. Once the first day. Twice the second day, and so on—every time the nurse thought I was asleep and it was safe for her to sneak out for some fool reason. Today I intend to walk."

"There's no hurry," Star said.

"Lower your voice," Tom ordered again, "and tell me something. Is Shad Traynor our guest at the moment?"

Shad froze. Tom *had* seen him, and now he wished he'd never been born. Abortions don't know how lucky they are!

"Of course not," Star said, "whatever made you ask that? As far as I know, Shad's in jail in New York."

If only that were true! Prison had never looked so good. There ought to be a law against the youthful-offender deal that had let him out too soon!

"Good," Tom said. "I don't mean good that he's in jail. I know how that hurts my dear Estelle, and I wholeheartedly support all her projects, of course. But Shad shouldn't be here when I lack full use of my capacities."

"Well, don't worry, he won't be around again for a long time, if ever."

131

"The reason I asked—there are two reasons, and well, the second reason is I thought I saw him late last night. Caught a glimpse of him peering in that window, a cigarette stuck to his lower lip as usual."

Star trembled. Could it be that Shad was out of jail—and here? She thought of George being robbed in the cabin—that was right up Shad's alley. But to reassure Tom, she said, "It must have been a dream."

A dream that'll keep me from getting old enough to die of lung cancer, Shad thought, longing for a cigarette.

"Then there was what Estelle told me when we were lying alone together," Tom said.

"What was that?"

"That she wanted to marry me again before they killed her. She said the first marriage was so long ago, the records kept in Heaven may have been mislaid, and she wanted to be sure a fresh copy got there ahead of her. I thought her fear of being killed was delirium. Then I thought I saw Shad and wasn't so sure."

"You mean you dreamed you saw Shad," Star said.

Then an idea, a plan he couldn't quite grasp began to form in Shad's mind. Nothing clear yet but a feeling of something forming, with a kernel of hope in it.

"Perhaps," said Tom. "But I want to discuss the dream with Harry as soon as possible. I don't know why he hasn't visited me this morning, but please call him and say I want to see him right away."

"All right," Star said, "in a few minutes. But I do think you should lie down now. Can I help?"

"Star, lying down is the one thing a man can always do by himself, even when he's dead."

Shad again heard sounds of considerable complaint from the bedsprings next door.

"Now phone Harry," Tom said again.

Now it became clear to Shad what he had to do to save his life. What Estelle had said about them killing her was for real. Ginelda must have got it for trying to pass something on, maybe to an outside partner—or else somebody who decided *she* made one partner too many.

Shad had to find out what Ginelda had known, or done, and prove it to the right people fast. Before Harry got back and began to wonder about the tracks he'd have to make from Ginelda's bathroom to the ladder that led to the room where he'd seen Star sleeping. If Harry got hold of him before he could prove someone else was the killer . . . God! The one thing worse than ordinary hanging would be whatever Harry would do to him!

CHAPTER XIII

"THAT WAS A lie about Naomi," Katinka told Harry, after he'd completed the dangerous maneuver of turning off Rose Island Road into the skidding traffic on Highway 42. "Everything's fine at home. We're going to Paul Ashton's."

"Why, for Christ's sake?"

"Because Dr. Clifford believes somebody is trying to murder Estelle."

"Good God! You mean she's been right all along? But why go to Paul instead of the police?"

"Well, he suggested it," said Katinka. "Dr. Clifford told me he spoke to Paul this morning. Paul wants us and the doctor to meet him at his house. No one else knows about this except Essie and Star, in case of emergency."

"Who does Clifford suspect?"

"No one yet. Nobody has any idea."

Nobody ... unless ... the thought ignited in Harry's mind—unless she told Tom last night! Trying to tell the rest of us hadn't helped her so far. As a last hope, she may have gathered her reserves to get to Tom while she still had her strength and possibly her memory, or enough of it, to tell him something vital as she lay in his arms—for how long no one knew—before they found her. And if the potential murderer was juggling these same thoughts, Tom isn't safe now either. He ought to go back to see Tom immediately, question him and protect him.

But they had already turned into the Ashton driveway, where Hettie Keller was murdered. Paul Ashton lived on five acres stuck like a small wedge between the Morgan wilderness and part of Harry's land. Harry coveted that wedge, though his cousin Paul made a nice neighbor.

Paul opened the front door before they could ring the bell and ushered them into the living room, where they settled themselves in easy chairs, facing a Christmasy view of his lawn through a picture window.

Paul was a tall, easy-moving man with dark eyes and very gray hair that took away nothing from his overall air of youthfulness. Or, as Estelle had put it, last summer, "He's grayer and has more lines in his face than most men in their fifties, but somehow he always looks brand-new. In a sophisticated manner, of course."

"I'd have come to your place," he said to Harry, "but it's safer here. With Betty Lou and the children in Florida, and Beulah on vacation too, no one can overhear us. No use saying much anyway until Dr. Clifford gets here."

A black-capped chickadee perched on a twig near the bird

feeder, fluffed its breast feathers and cocked its head to fix a beady eye on the human habitat, so well displayed for it behind glass.

Harry didn't feel any urge to say a word. His mother was the target of some maniac. He clasped his large, farm-worn hands together, his whole self centered in them, with an imagined throat between them. He had killed in war, and could again.

He shook his head "no" to the fragrant cup of coffee Paul offered. He couldn't release his hands, digging painfully into each other.

Dr. Clifford arrived within minutes, his well-shaved face pink with embarrassment, his expression one of pained incredulity. "I should have realized what was happening sooner," he said. "I was awake all night pondering the oddities of this case. Then this morning I had a pre-office-hours conference about it with all my partners. For the third time this week—we've been puzzled all week. Without medication, you see, a toxic psychosis shouldn't drag on like this, and her kind of derangement has significant features that don't fit with a diagnosis of senile paranoia."

"Like what?" Harry asked.

"Her unswerving belief in her family, for one thing."

"A real point," Paul commented. "I've heard the advanced paranoid usually attacks his nearest and dearest first, before tackling the rest of the world."

"That's usually true," Dr. Clifford agreed. "And it's stuck in my craw for a couple of days. This morning, it hit us all: a crime is being committed. I'm afraid we were a bit slow in suspecting it."

137

"If I could get my hands on him, the bastard," Harry muttered, digging his nails still deeper into his own flesh.

"One fact has been nudging at my mind for some time," Dr. Clifford went on. "During the Christmas holidays—before Christmas—the druggist told me someone at the Morgans had ordered an injectible protein substance he didn't have in stock, and a syringe. I told him I hadn't prescribed anything of the kind, but he said he'd already delivered the syringe. I asked Ginelda the next day to find out who ordered the stuff, and she reported no one in the house knew anything about it."

"Even if the druggist thought he knew who ordered it, that wouldn't help," Paul said. "No jury'd buy identification of a voice over the phone."

"What about the syringe?" Harry questioned.

"I didn't push the matter," Dr. Clifford said. "A nurse must have a syringe as part of her equipment, and would have sense enough not to use it without a doctor's orders. The needle marks would be a dead giveaway in a case like this, and there aren't any on Mrs. Morgan, so I don't know why I even brought up the matter." He hesitated, and then went on talking more to himself than to Harry. "All I know for certain is that I have a patient who's evidently been getting drugs I didn't prescribe, and she's been getting them for some time. The dosage hasn't been large enough to be fatal yet, but if she continues getting it, it soon will."

"When do we call the police?" Harry asked.

"Essie agreed we should give Paul the time he needs—a few hours, a day, two if necessary," Dr. Clifford said. "Meanwhile, Essie herself is as good a guardian as we could

138

get for the moment. And the most welcome to your mother. When I picked her up at the Brown Hotel, I told her to be sure your mother isn't left alone for a second, except with you, Katinka or Star."

"Why don't we put her in a hospital?" Harry asked. "And ... " He'd been about to say "and Tom too," but stopped himself cold, because Tom would be safer if no one realized—*no one at all*—that he might know something "they" didn't want known.

"That was my first impulse," Dr. Clifford said, "but Paul said to wait."

"Why?" Harry asked, staring intently at Paul. "Wouldn't she be safer there, entirely surrounded by new people? And with several doctors to check on her?"

"Dr. Clifford says she'll be all right at home so long as a member of the family is always with her," Paul said. "And if no one can get at her from outside her room, through her food or drink."

"What about the syringe?" Harry asked.

"Nobody can use it on her with the family watching," Paul said.

"When will she be well enough to tell us what's been going on?" Harry asked Dr. Clifford.

"She may come to in an hour or several hours. There may be a few days' hangover of confusion—drug-induced amnesia."

"But who would want to kill her?" Harry asked, "And why?"

"To get her money!" Paul said. "Remember, there's over two million involved."

"How much is Ginelda getting?" Harry asked.

"But she's been with the family twenty years!" Katinka said. "What about Shad Traynor or one of the other baby cobras?"

"They're all in the will," Paul said, "for five thousand each. Ginelda is in for ten. But Estelle told me she'd apprised you of the intent of her will, if not the specific provisions."

"She did," said Harry, "and I was thinking Ginelda may be in a hurry to get that ten. Let's fire her and the whole gaggle of nurses. Get new ones. Only I still can't see why we don't put Mother in the hospital." Perhaps he ought to insist on it with no more palaver. Suspicion of Dr. Clifford, and Paul too, was spreading in him like a dark stain. His mother had probably left money to some hungry philanthropy Dr. Clifford was interested in. He'd bet half his share she had. He intended to have another doctor look at his mother, and soon.

Paul looked at him as if he could read his mind. "Give me the time I asked for," he pleaded. "I want to talk to the druggist, see what he's sent to the house so far this month, and last month. And get the lowdown on each of the nurses, and go over all household bills—all bills of any kind, paid and unpaid. You never know where a lead'll turn up."

"To hell with leads!" Harry said. "I'd like to kill whoever is doing it, but I want even more to have my mother safe." And Tom, too, he thought. What the hell was Essie thinking of, giving Paul so much say-so.

"I see your point," Paul said. "If only we could be sure every suspect is *in* the house. It seems likely it's an inside job. . . . "

"Then let's throw out the goddamned 'likely' *now!*" Harry said.

"You don't understand. It may not be entirely an inside job. An outsider, aiming to get hold of the big money, somehow, could be directing it from a safe distance. With Ginelda or one of the nurses as a paid tool. If there is such a person, we must find him—or her—too, if we want to keep Aunt Estelle really safe. And I have a better chance of finding out if I can work on my own for a while, without doing anything to alert the enemy and put them on their guard. I'm going to ask Frank Wertz to help." Wertz was the best criminal lawyer in Louisville.

"I see what you mean," Harry said, aware that his voice sounded as ominous as the grinding of ice against a dam. "There really could be an outsider. Like the Texas millionaire I read about. He was smothered by a butler in the pay of his lawyer and heir." Harry turned toward the window to catch the eye of the chickadee.

"But you aren't in the will, are you, Paul?" Katinka asked.

"My children are, for one thousand each," Paul said, "as a contribution to their college education."

Or as far as we know now, for a larger bequest, Harry thought. It could be he's "forgotten" the exact amounts.

"Shad Traynor could have made a deal with one of the haircurler tribe," Katinka said, "offered to split, fifty-fifty."

Paul shook his head. "Shad might snatch the wedding ring off her finger, but he wouldn't have the patience or the subtlety for this kind of crime."

"He stole three cars in nine months," Katinka said.

"I stole dozens, with a gang of friends when I was six,"

141

Paul said. "Little plastic ones from the five-and-ten. But I didn't grow up a hardened criminal."

"What you're saying is there's a crime but no criminal," Harry said. And thought: Who said you didn't grow up a hardened criminal? Essie? She didn't count. She'd always had a slight crush on her cousin. . . .

"There's a criminal, all right," Paul said, "but I don't think Shad is the one."

"There are five outsiders in the house right now," Harry said. "Ginelda, and four nurses."

None of this gathering yet knew of the sixth outsider— George.

Paul sighed. "They are to be kept outsiders from now on. Kept outside Aunt Estelle's room and away from any food or drink of hers. One of you," he looked at Harry and Katinka, "can drive into Louisville in the event she needs anything special."

"And she does. She needs nightgowns urgently. I'll go, Harry—and go now," said Katinka. "I know just what kind to get her, the kind that open down the front, easy to slip into."

"Fine," Paul said. "All food for her—and I mean everything—must be bought by and prepared by one of you. Don't use anything lying around, no matter what."

"Ginelda's going to be asking questions," warned Harry.

"Tell her Dr. Clifford wants Star to fix Estelle some tempting dishes she learned in her Cordon Bleu cooking classes. Everyone knows Aunt Estelle goes for French food. Or any other excuse you can think of."

"Yes, and get bottled water," Dr. Clifford said.

"And don't confide in anyone while you're shopping," Paul warned Katinka.

142

"Don't worry! I was born not talking. Nazis were always in earshot."

"Another thing," Paul said as Katinka put on her bright-red coat, "be careful if you have to make any phone calls from the Morgan house. The cabin phone is safe, but the house has an extension in every room."

Katinka laughed harshly. "I learned that kind of precaution before I learned long division, when my playmates were being made into soap." She turned and hurried out of the room, leaving Dr. Clifford and Paul startled both at her vehemence and at her brusque departure. But Harry knew she was hurrying away to keep them from seeing the tears that always came to her eyes when she thought of her childhood.

Harry watched her go, and then turned to Dr. Clifford and Paul. Not saying anything. Just thinking, and hating his thoughts. He saw what Paul had in mind now. He'd fixed it so it would appear that any further attempt against Estelle would have to be made by him, his wife, his sister, or Star. In that way, neither Ginelda nor any one of the nurses could be held responsible if anything went wrong. It stood to reason that the worried physician and the suave attorney were thinking it must be one of the relatives and had cooked up a good plan to find out which one. Unless they were the would-be murderers. Dr. Clifford would have access to the sickroom, or a confederate among the women who did, and Paul might be the "outsider."

"Don't worry, Harry," Paul said. "After I've checked on a few people, we *will* call the police."

Harry looked straight into the eyes of his cousin. The gaze that met his was serene, trusting. There was nothing in Paul's demeanor to suggest he could be guilty himself, or that he suspected Harry was. Which proved nothing except that composure under stress is part of a good lawyer's stock in trade.

The phone rang. It was Star, asking for Harry. She told him Tom wanted to see him, and Essie wanted him on the premises, too. For protection. "I'm on my way," Harry told her. He turned to Paul and Dr. Clifford and said, "Star says Essie wants me back at the house—it's nothing special."

"I can drive you, since Katinka's taken the car," Dr. Clifford offered.

"Thanks, I prefer to walk. Cutting through the woods, I'll make it in no time."

The narrow tip of the wedge formed by Ashton's acres ended on a hilltop with Harry's flat fields to the right and a steep hill of Morgan wilderness to the left. Left, he remembered, is associated with sinister. So are dark forests, and though the day was sunny, precious little light got through to ground level in the thick woods ahead. At the bottom of this dark, precipitous slope, and invisible from the top, there was a narrow strip of private road leading from Rose Island Road to the Morgan house.

Harry plunged toward that private road by the shortest route, ignoring most ground-level obstacles between the intrusive apex of Ashton's wedge and his father's road. The only obstacles he couldn't ignore were the trees. He would have crashed into them if he hadn't gone around them, inwardly cursing each one of the scores in his path for not being somewhere else.

His stride was swifter than he intended, and less cautious,

so great was his hurry. The fresh dry powdery snow covering a layer of ice made footing treacherous, and Harry slipped and slid with each giant step. He accepted this as fate, maintaining his balance with dextrous use of his stick and strong, flexible muscles. And some unappreciated help from the constant zigzagging made necessary by the trees.

Halfway down the hill there was a natural clearing, a small glade where the sun, still rising—Harry's watch said 9:30 A.M.—reached down to the virgin snow, creating an unexpected expanse of white touched with melting gold, the more beautiful because of the forest darkness that rimmed it.

"A 'jewel in an Ethiop's ear,' " he thought, and no trees to block his way as he ran across it. He was almost to the road, and then home. Home, where a man's presence was sorely needed. Not Tom. A whole man.

His right foot caught on something camouflaged by the snow, sending him sprawling head first. As he lifted his face out of the snow, he remembered the great oak tree struck by lightning last summer that had fallen across the glade and still lay there, hidden now by blankets of sleet and snow. Damned cold blankets, even here in the sun, out of the wind. He drew his spread-eagled arms and legs under his body to raise himself up and hurry on.

It was only when he couldn't rise that he realized his right leg hadn't responded like its mate to his mental order to get going. It lay limp and twisted. He put all his strength into a mighty effort to draw it under him, alongside the other. The rest of his body was obedient to his will, but not his right leg. He roared orders at it, in unconscious imitation of Tom, but that didn't help, either.

The leg was broken. It didn't hurt yet, accident anesthesia,

145

but it was broken. He was helpless in the killing cold, halfway between Paul's and his father's house. Cries for help would be a waste of time. When he was missed, he'd be quickly found. His footprints in the snow from Paul's to the glade left a trail easily followed, if it didn't snow again.

But Paul would go to his office. Katinka was nearing Louisville by now. No one would pass this way by chance. It would be a long time, quite a long time, before anyone thought to look for him.

Walking, he'd been comfortably warm in his winter clothing. Lying here, motionless, he felt the cold begin to seep into his bones. To survive, he had to get moving. He started propelling himself forward, vigorously pulling with his arms and pushing with the good leg, while the other dragged behind.

He had lives to save—his mother's, his father's, his own. And all that damned leg could do about it was start hurting. Soon it had every corpuscle screaming for tender, loving care. He continued doggedly dragging himself on. Nearly a mile to go; half of it to the private road, and the other half mostly winding uphill. If only this were happening in the Alps, he thought, all but seeing a rescuing St. Bernard come toward him. But false hope would be death in his situation.

Finally he hobbled and dragged himself to the road, crawled through the fence and a shallow ditch to get to the middle of the road, where going would be easier. But in doing so he felt his ankle on the broken leg drag across something jagged beneath the snow. Once on the road he stopped, pulled up the pants leg and saw the ankle was not only badly cut but bleeding profusely.

He was hurt and losing blood, helpless and in a hurry. Yet

he could go no farther at the moment. He could only lie in the road, too weak even to call for help.

And almost irrationally, he thought of the lock he'd removed from Estelle's bathroom door, with the best of intentions. Now he felt he'd deprived her of even that refuge.

CHAPTER XIV

KATINKA WAS ANXIOUS to finish her shopping duties and get back to the Morgan home and then on to her children, so she shopped efficiently and quickly, though she was very tired. She'd lain awake most of the previous night, but then she was used to sleeplessness. Had been ever since her childhood in Amsterdam, when she'd watched Nazi soldiers march her favorite playmate, Sarah, toward waiting trucks. Sarah, her mother and father walking on either side of her, had been dressed in her birthday dress with bright-red ribands on each of her shining dark braids. And now, whenever she was over-tired, the memory of Sarah and her parents haunted her.

But she mustn't be tired today—too much to do. First of all, she bought special foods, bottled water, some produce that she hoped would tempt Estelle as she recuperated, some canned goods that could not be tampered with by others—enough supplies to last for a reasonable siege, if necessary. Then she went to Stewart's for nightgowns.

She soon found four pretty and practical nylon gowns that would be perfect for Estelle. Then she saw another gown, made of real silk. It was probably not appropriate, though it was styled right, with loose sleeves and open down the front. Katinka had never bought real silk for herself, partly because it was so expensive, and partly because it was hard to take care of, but the beauty of this one tugged at her. Once when Naomi was dangerously ill in the hospital, at the age of three months, Estelle had impulsively bought a fantastically expensive handmade blanket to wrap her in. It was the antibiotics and the transfusions that saved the child's life, of course, but the enfolding beauty of the blanket had been what the grandmother could give, her attempt to convey the preciousness of Naomi's fragile life to the doctors, the nurses, to Naomi's own infant self.

"I'll pay cash for this and take it," Katinka said, pointing to the real silk that would be her special gift to Estelle. "The other four will be a charge and take. Charge to Mrs. Tom Morgan, Prospect, Kentucky 40059."

"My goodness! More gowns for Mrs. Morgan? It's none of my business, of course, but how can she use so many?"

"So many?" Katinka looked at the salesgirl in surprise. "Well, she's ill and can't wear anything but nightgowns, so it's kind of cheering to have a variety."

"Oh, sure—a change for dinner and all. That's what I did myself, when I had my operation. But six last Thursday, six the week before, and six the week before *that!*"

"But these are the first new gowns she's had in several years! You must be thinking of someone else."

"No, I'm not. Like I said, this woman called in last week and the week before and the week before that, and each time she charged six gowns, all of them same style, in satin, to Mrs. Tom Morgan in Prospect. 'Charge and send,' she said. Three sixes is eighteen and now you're getting five more—that's twenty-three gowns in about three weeks, if the one you're paying cash for is for her too. Otherwise, twenty-two."

Essie and Mrs. Purdie had cut Estelle out of her soiled gown just this morning and she, Katinka, had hastily altered an old one, not knowing any new ones had been bought for her already. Where were they?

"While you're wrapping them for me, I'll make a phone call," Katinka said.

Paul Ashton was startled. "Eighteen nightgowns? And none in the house? I don't know what it'll prove, but I'll certainly look into it. Let me know any other oddities that turn up."

The next oddity was George.

It was near the lunch hour when Katinka returned from Louisville. She went to the cabin to see if Star was there and ask her to help unload the car. "Come in," Star called when she knocked. Katinka opened the door and was assailed by the warm aromas of cheese soufflé, lamb chops, and chocolate soufflé. During her summer course in culinary art, Star had become a soufflé expert.

The food and several bottles of Coke were spread out on a bridge table in front of a big armchair, with Star and a young man cuddled into it. A snug fit.

The young man struggled to his feet at the sight of Katinka, all but overturning the table. Star, still sitting, holding one of his hands in both of hers, said, "Katinka, this is George, my ... fiancé. He's staying here with me."

"I'm glad to meet you," George said.

"Katinka is my aunt," Star explained, leaning her head against George's thigh.

Katinka offered him her hand in uncertain welcome—another outsider. Maybe he and Star ... but that was unthinkable.

"He flew down last night," Star said, "to help us keep Estelle from being murdered."

"And to be robbed," he added ruefully.

But Star gave Katinka no time to take that fact in. "Of course," she said, "he has to work on his senior thesis, too."

"Well, he can help now by unloading the car with me," Katinka said. "I can use him and Harry both."

"Harry isn't here," Star said, "or at your house either. I've been trying to reach him. But George'll be all you need." Her tone implied George would always be all anyone could ever need.

Katinka watched them help each other on with their coats, in an enchanted daze of touching, of bodies brushing, of breath-mingling closeness.

"Didn't you bring a scarf?" Star asked.

"No, I left in a hurry. Anyway, I don't need it."

"Yes, you do." She took a long, woolly brown-and-beige muffler of hers from a hanger. "It's cold out. I'll lend you this."

As she put it around his neck, her fingertips explored his ear lobes, his hair, and the back and sides of his neck. His hands rested lightly on her hips for a fleeting second. Then they all went out, Star and George walking side by side, arm in arm, their shoulders and thighs frequently brushing as if they had invisible magnets inside them, irresistibly drawing them together.

For unloading and carrying cartons and gallon bottles of distilled water to Estelle's room, with Star directing his every move, George was useful. Katinka remembered herself and Harry in Holland, dancing on ice skates to music during the first Christmas of their love. It surprised her to see that carrying heavy loads to a sickroom could be an equally ecstatic experience.

"Have *you* seen Harry lately?" Star asked Katinka, as she and George grasped a particularly heavy box.

"No. He must be attending to something in a far acre of the farm, a tractor with a screw loose, or a sick cow. It would be totally in character for the cows, the whole herd, to come down with a virus at a time like this."

"Maybe," Star said, "but Harry ought to be here anyway. There are vets for cows, and I did tell him Tom wants him. I called him at Paul's."

"I don't understand," Katinka said. "I guess he'll show up and even have a good reason for the delay."

CHAPTER XV

THE ANIMAL AROUND the man's neck moved. It must have been the one that screamed in the trap. Yes ... she remembered that, remembered hearing the scream. But where? And when?

She turned her head on the pillow in an effort to see past the man who seemed to be placing one big block on top of another. The animal tried to pull its paw out of the cold bite of the trap. She should attempt to help it, but how could she, the way things were shifting around her in this storeroom? Yes, that's what this place was—it must be a storeroom. All that stuff piled up against walls—boxes, cartons, bottles. . . .

Once she'd lived in a place where there were no traps. Tom didn't allow them. A sign on the great boulder at the entrance said so. It said in big letters, very black on white: NO HUNTING OR FISHING ALLOWED. TRESPASSERS WILL BE PROSECUTED TO THE FULL EXTENT OF THE LAW. TOM MORGAN.

But now they had dumped her in this storeroom with discarded things, and money wouldn't influence them to let her out. She knew that. Anyway, she didn't have any money anymore. They'd taken the purse and she didn't care.

"Jimmy crack corn and I don't care."

"What?" someone asked, quite loud.

She answered louder, "Jimmy crack corn and I don't care. Jimmy crack corn—I don't care, I don't care, I don't care!"

Then suddenly she did care, couldn't help it. "Look, look," she cried, pointing to the aquarium. "For God's sake, do something!"

"Do what, Estelle?" someone asked. Not the man with the animal around his neck—a woman's voice.

"The frog—make them stop—they're crucifying it."

"There's no frog in the aquarium, Estelle. It's only sea-weed you see, Nothing is being hurt."

Nothing is being hurt. Cherishing the thought, Estelle saw a quiet forest path. Tom was walking along it with a young girl beside him. A girl she had once known. Estelle French was her name. She was wearing a picture hat and an ankle-length white dress with a blue sash. She was in love and about to be married. To be Estelle Morgan for the rest of her natural life. Natural?

There were four people in the storeroom with her. One was a man, neither Tom nor Harry, and three women, all pretty, like Estelle French. It must be a party, but this was a queer place to have it. Maybe that's why no one was particularly dressed up. A party in a proper place would be better—in a room with candles and flowers and the girls wearing dresses like Estelle used to wear when she was

156

dancing a Viennese waltz with Tom. They ... the dresses ... they—they!

She began to tremble. *They* don't go to parties. They— "Jimmy crack corn," she managed again, looking at the youngest girl—"and I don't care." The girl came nearer. It was—Star!

"Star, take me away from here. Don't let them keep me in this dingy storeroom. Star ... I'm ... I don't belong here ... I'm ... I'm ... I'm Estelle French Morgan, Mrs. Tom Morgan. I know I am!"

"Of course you are. You're Estelle Morgan and you're in your own room." It was the older woman who said that. It was her daughter, Essie. Star, Essie, Katinka—and that other figure.

The animal around his neck had changed into a scarf. But she still didn't want him in her room, didn't want anyone she didn't know and couldn't trust. Not even Dr. Clifford ... Clifford ... doctor ... shots—and the cold whirling dark.

"I'm not taking any more. Get out of here!" she screamed at George.

He went out and Star followed him.

She called after them: "Star, tell him—no hunting allowed. He'll be vigorously prosecuted. Tell him!"

Then two women in white dresses came in.

"Out!" she cried.

"Mrs. Purdie and Trudy are going to change your sheets," Essie said, "and get you into a beautiful new nightgown before lunch."

"It takes two to do it without hurting our poor arm," Mrs. Purdie said gently.

157

"We just want our whole room freshened up," the other one said, the one who smiled like a crocodile—Trudy.

"No!"

"Now, now, we won't feel anything," Trudy crocodile said.

"You *know* I never hurt you," Mrs. Purdie said. "It's not quite fair to act as if I ever did, is it?"

"We've just been having bad dreams," the crocodile said soothingly, "so we don't realize how gentle our Mrs. Purdie is." They converged on the bed, but Katinka and Essie came close too, and that made her feel all right.

They were gentle with the sheets, and leaning back against a fresh pillowcase, she told herself firmly that the dead baby boy she was looking at certainly wasn't there.

But the sight was so pitiful she couldn't tear her eyes away. Besides, wherever she looked, the infant was there, as though he floated from place to place with her gaze. Better the poor little thing should stay on the soft cushion of the armchair than have to lie on the hard mantelpiece or just hang in the air. Did Essie and Katinka see him? They had turned to look in the same direction as she. Mrs. Purdie and crocodile too.

"What do you see?" she cried before she could stop herself.

"Nothing. Not a thing. Nothing at all," several voices answered.

She should have known. If they'd seen the baby boy, they would have screamed. All of them. Even the crocodile. And Essie would be telephoning a doctor. Essie always knew the best thing to do. But Essie must *not* know—just as she mustn't know about that cancer thirty years ago—mustn't know that she, Estelle, was seeing things that weren't there. She'd be afraid that it meant craziness and that her children would inherit it. Bad seed.

But that wasn't it. Shots had something to do with it, something to do with that poor little baby boy lying naked and dead on the seat of the easy chair. Maybe if he were wrapped in a blanket and warmed in her arms, he would start breathing. But sometimes nothing will make them start—not warming, not love, not prayer. Her third child never started. Poor little boy, born but never mothered. So lonely. The thought tore at her as the child did when he came out of her body and didn't breathe.

If that one on the chair—but he wasn't the baby she had lost ... he wasn't real. She could see that in the faces around her.

Hail Mary, Mother of God, she thought, please take care of all the babies that don't breathe, real or unreal. She wasn't Catholic or even what you'd call religious, but it would be good, wonderful, to believe in a divine love, all-embracing. A love that would embrace even ... them.

The Mother of God had taken the baby away, gathering him into her arms, as she had the one that would have been named Tom if he'd been born alive. People could believe something like that without being crazy. And she was not going to stay crazy. They couldn't make her.

She shuddered with intensified knowledge of them waiting to push her under once more, with a thrust that would keep her from coming up again, and prevent her ever remembering, telling.

Memory was gathering inside her like a fresh clear current, washing off the slimy mud of confusion that coated her

159

brain. She would become herself again, take care of Tom, drive, babysit, if . . .

Blackness, cold black depths. What she least wanted to think about was smothering blackness. But from deep within her came a certainty that she must. She must remember about the black purse.

Star came in again, bringing a tray with a slightly wilted gardenia on it. The crocodile put a surprisingly soft arm under her shoulders to help her sit up, and Mrs. Purdie piled the linen on the cartons on the cedar chest and helped fix pillows at her back. The mirror over the dresser reflected the room, overcrowded with a lot of cartons and water jugs that didn't belong in it, but still familiar—same wallpaper, same curtains, faded to a lovely shade of old rose. The smell of breakfast coffee—or was it lunch—made just the right counterpoint to the sweetness from the gardenia.

The drip of melting snow from the eaves promised violets, crocuses, and new corn and white lambs in the fields she would pass driving from here to Louisville if . . . if she remembered enough now, while Katinka, Essie and Star were here with her. This was as safe a time as any to let her mind sink into its hideous depths, break free of the cobwebby amnesia. Pills. Pills dissolved in coffee. Pills she didn't want. Why had she taken them? It was still too much for her.

Mrs. Purdie gathered up the linen from the cartons on the chest and said to Essie, "I'll take all this down for Ginelda to put in the washing machine when she wakens. She was up all night, remember. And then I'll straighten up the back bedroom a bit."

"Straighten it thoroughly," Essie said.

Mrs. Purdie stiffened but said politely, "Very well. I think we're past the crisis, but call me if you need me."

160

"We're going to be all right," the crocodile said, "but Mrs. Purdie and I will be right here ready to help if we have even the teensiest relapse."

Finally they were gone. Star, too. She could hear their footsteps on the stairs going down.

The food on her tray—scrambled eggs and bacon, with café au lait, mostly au lait. If she ate and thought at the same time, it might steady the thoughts, she decided. Aloud she said, " 'For a handful of silver he left us,/For a riband to stick in his coat.' "

"What?" Katinka asked.

"Odd," Estelle said, "there wasn't even a riband in it for them. No . . . *not* them . . . they . . . she. It was just a she."

"Who?" Katinka asked, leaning over the bed. Essie stood perfectly still by the dresser she'd been straightening.

"Sometimes she seems to have three heads. But that's only when nothing looks the way it is because of what they're doing to me. I mean she."

"Who?" Katinka asked again.

"Them—her. I know what I'm saying. My mind is clear, Katinka."

"Of course. Just tell us who you mean by 'she'."

"As clear as anyone's. I know my algebra and Latin—factoring, the ablative absolute, and poetry."

"Tell us who you mean by 'she'," Katinka insisted.

"Let her just talk," Essie whispered.

"But she keeps digressing."

"Leave her alone, please!"

"Tom and I used to memorize poetry together, in English, Spanish, and French. '*Ou sont les neiges d'antan*—Where are the snows of yesteryear?' I don't remember how to put that in Spanish, but I'm going to stop them from making this the last snow I see. When my time comes—but I will not let them hurry it with their needles—if I don't drink the coffee, she uses the needle. Sometimes she just uses the needle anyway," she rambled on.

Essie moved closer to the bed, to Katinka's side. Estelle could see they were both listening, *hearing* at last.

"You see, natural dying won't be frightening," she told them. "I don't think it will be. But the kind of death that's forced on you, when you scream for help and no one hears— when someone comes and you can't explain because your mind's too deep in the mire. . . . "

"It's all right now. It's over, you're safe," Katinka said.

"I know she isn't in the room now," Estelle said, looking around her thoughtfully.

"Who?" Katinka asked.

"Who?" Essie echoed. "Is it Ginelda?"

"Not Ginelda. She was going to call Paul Ashton for me."

"You're sure?" Essie asked.

"I'm sure of that much. But that's not enough and it's horrible to go back." She closed her eyes. "I have to get back to before the one face became three. To before you came, Essie. It began when the black purse was stuck in the chest, deep into the bottom under all the blankets. Star didn't think to look there, but that's where it is, only the money is gone. The whole three hundred dollars that Harry put in. She took it all."

"Who took it?" Katinka asked.

"Let me think."

Katinka looked toward the chest and then, inquiringly, at Essie. Essie nodded. Katinka removed two cartons from the top of the chest, opened it, releasing an odor of clean wool and mothballs into the room. She knelt on the floor, thrust her right arm deep into the chest and felt along its bottom, under the blankets. An expression of triumph came into her face and she jerked her arm free. The worn, outsized black purse was in her hand. She fumbled nervously with the clasp, finally got it open.

Estelle said with certainty, "The money is gone."

"Yes, it is," Katinka said and took a piece of folded paper out of the purse.

"That's not mine," Estelle said.

Katinka unfolded the paper. "This handwriting is pretty shaky—doesn't look much like hers," she said to Essie, who was looking over her shoulder.

Then Essie started reading out loud: "To Ginelda for her kindness—fifty dollars. To Tom's three nurses, for their kind-ness—seventy-five dollars each. To Mrs. Purdie, for her kindness—seventy-five dollars."

"But that comes to fifty dollars more than Harry put in the purse," Katinka said, puzzled.

"They were in too much of a hurry to add carefully," Estelle said, and added, "but they ... she ... didn't give it away like that."

"Who?" Katinka asked.

"I'll remember soon. But I need to lie down again, first. With you here with me, always with me."

"Don't worry," Essie said, "one of us will be here around the clock."

Katinka took the tray and Essie helped Estelle lie down. She closed her eyes and found herself in a kind of darkness she'd almost forgotten about, the warmly enfolding kind that leads into peaceful sleep.

"Try to remember," Essie urged.

"Maybe I'll wake up knowing," Estelle said. "I can't try anymore now." She couldn't, just couldn't.

In the downstairs hall, Star gave George a brief, violent hug and said, "Go out to the cabin by the front door. That way there won't be any danger of Tom seeing you. I don't want him to see you until I've told him we're going to be married. Even then, I don't want him to know you've been in the cabin all night. He'd never believe our story—or know that I'm too worried about Uncle Harry to do *anything but* worry."

"What could have happened to him?" George asked. "And to my money and watch?" He shook his head. Things were pretty weird when they didn't even want him to call the police about his robbery. "Take plenty of time with Tom," he said. "Get him to accept me. Meanwhile, I'll get something done on my thesis."

"All right. I'll give you an hour. I'm going to make a special broth for Estelle, before I approach Tom in his den."

CHAPTER XVI

PAUL ASHTON HAD barely glanced at the morning paper, but one small news item had caught his eye and nudged at his mind with nagging persistence. He wanted to concentrate on his Aunt Estelle's predicament and the millions that had doubtless caused it. But that miserable scrap of news about a seventy-four-year-old man being knocked unconscious and robbed of two dollars and seventy-seven cents kept distracting him from his thoughtful re-reading of his aunt's last will and testament, in search of more material for Frank Wertz to consider.

He sighed and inked out the $2.77 that had appeared again among the doodles on his memo pad, and tried to keep his mind on the will and the few facts he had to go on: eighteen satin nightgowns charged to Mrs. Tom Morgan by a woman in the Morgan home; no new nightgowns found in the house except those purchased this morning by Katinka;

the "for her kindness" notes with an error in simple arithmetic, found in Estelle's emptied handbag; several good recommendations obtained by his secretary for each of the Morgan nurses from families who had used their services in the last two years.

The matter of the nightgowns was the least puzzling. They probably had been ordered by someone in the house, certainly by a dishonest person, knowing that all such packages were automatically placed in the back room that had been used temporarily to store things. Then the person who ordered the items could easily manage to get them out of the house.

The "for her kindness" notes he put aside; there seemed to be no clue to that problem.

Next he concentrated on the names of the nurses and their records. His secretary had typed them on a long sheet of yellow paper, and under each name had typed the names of their employers in that period. These added up to four grateful patients now in good health, and the surviving relatives of twelve other patients with nothing but good to say of the nursing care their dear ones had received before passing on.

It struck Paul that the death rate was rather high, so he called Dr. Clifford. Eight of the twelve dead patients named on the yellow sheet had been Clifford's. So was one of those still living.

"I have a list of some of your patients here with a mortality rate that makes me feel we ought to avoid further use of the Morgan nurses . . . " and Paul managed a less than sincere tone of jocularity, " . . . or change physicians."

"Would you read me the list?" The doctor had no sense of humor.

Paul complied.

"They were all terminal cases," said the doctor, "kept alive by excellent nursing care for weeks longer than I would have thought possible. Even Burnett, who's still alive, shouldn't have made it. The odds were ninety percent against him."

Paul then called the doctors who had been in charge of the cases of the others who had succumbed. Their reports were equally reassuring.

Again he scratched $2.77 on his memo pad and studied the list of Estelle's heirs. Tom had refused to be among them, said he'd rather go on welfare than live off his wife's money.

The widespread belief in the family was that Estelle would leave a bit over two million dollars. She regretted their knowing that much, since she considered unearned wealth immoral. At least in such large amounts. So she had seen to it that only Paul and her bankers were aware that the entire estate was near five million. She had left two million to each of her children and divided the fifth among the cobras, Ginelda, Paul's children, and various medical research projects, some probably recommended by Dr. Clifford.

When Dr. Clifford first called him early in the morning, Paul had immediately engaged Jerry Kountz, the best detective he knew, to find out all he could about the recent movements of the three apparently rehabilitated cobras—how they'd been spending their time in the last few weeks.

Again he wrote $2.77 and again irritably scratched it out. There was a time in the life of each of the cobras when he

167

might have killed for $2.77, if he'd been big enough. Now none of them would, not even Shad Traynor. Shad would want a bigger return on the risk. Shad was "unstable," as Aunt Estelle would put it, but not stupid. Like me, he thought, as he found himself writing $2.77 for about the fiftieth time on his memo pad, as though he were a tool of automatic writing.

The phone rang and Paul answered. It was Essie. "Listen," she said, "I'm calling from the back bedroom, so Katinka won't hear me. I don't want to worry her, but I think something's happened to Harry. He isn't here, and it's a long time since he left your house. Star says she told him it was urgent—that Tom wanted him here."

"I'll call Skaggs," Paul said. "He'll trace him from my house, find him in ten minutes if he's in those woods."

On a hunch he first called Martha Sneedon's store and sure enough found Sheriff Skaggs there—a far better place for taking the pulse of the community than his own office.

"I'll find him, and fast," Skaggs promised.

When Shad consulted George's watch for the hundredth time, it was twelve o'clock. He could not remain under the bed another minute; he carefully crawled out and just made it to Ginelda's bathroom in time. Now if he could only get to the kitchen for something to eat; he was starving. But when he was thinking of the food, he heard someone enter the kitchen, and so he slid quickly back under the bed in the event they entered Ginelda's room.

Then at twelve thirty-five, he decided he had to make a positive move of some sort. They wouldn't leave Ginelda to sleep forever without checking on her. He squirmed out from under the bed and tried to keep his eyes averted from poor Ginelda, lying in what he and only one other knew was perpetual sleep. He peeked out the window and saw Katinka, Star, and the young fellow he'd robbed carrying packages into the house. What was that all about?

Then he heard voices beginning to fill the kitchen. That meant his only way out of the house was through Ginelda's window. There were now enough tracks in the snow that his would not be noticed. He opened the window quietly, then fingered his switchblade in the event he met anyone. But anyone knifed would only scream, raising an alarm. His glance caught a heavy gold-plated statuette on the highboy. It was a skating trophy Harry had won, and when he lost interest in it, he passed it on to Ginelda, who had greatly admired the piece. Shad lifted it, tested it for weight. It was easy to grasp and small enough to carry.

He took the statuette and was immediately glad he did, for before he was completely out the window, he again saw the fellow who had just been helping Star and Katinka with their packages. The man stopped when he saw Shad, seemed about to smile in greeting—and then his expression changed and he charged. Thinking about his money and watch, Shad guessed, and quickly jerked his leg out the window. When the man was close enough, Shad swung the statuette. It caught the man in the middle of the forehead, stopped him dead in his tracks before he fell backward into the snow. Shad took a hurried glance at the gash and thanked his luck that it was not as deep a wound as the iron had made in Ginelda's head. But it was sure as hell enough of a blow to keep this guy out for some time. If he wasn't dead. Shad shuddered at that thought. Killing was not his thing.

But no matter if the man was knocked out or dead, Shad knew he had to move on. His aim was to get into the main house, see Tom, give his spiel and then split.

CHAPTER XVII

IT TOOK TOM Morgan several seconds to grasp the fact that the figure in the doorway was no apparition. His vision of Shad—flesh, blood, and cigarette smoke—hadn't been a dream after all! He was right here on the sun porch. Where else had he been? Was Estelle safe? Tom jerked and twisted to a sitting position and swung his feet to the floor. Weakness forced him to grip the bars of his bed to keep from falling.

"Play it cool," Shad said, in a low voice, hardly above a whisper. "I got big news for you about Estelle ... and Ginelda."

Tom tightened his grip on the bed rail, tightened his whole body, summoning his strength. The last psychiatric report from that school had suggested Shad might become dangerous to Estelle. Last night she herself had told him someone was trying to murder her. And there was no one in the house now except helpless women, himself, and this monster.

"Take it easy," Shad said, coming toward him, one hand behind his back.

Let him come closer, close enough for me to get my hands on him, Tom prayed. If I could fall on top of him, I could strangle him. . . .

"Don't blow a fuse trying to charge me," Shad said. "You'll never make it. And don't start roaring. Just listen."

Tom had no intention of roaring. He could see Shad was trembling, keyed up to the snapping point, if he hadn't already snapped. Any word, any gesture that alarmed him could precipitate disaster. Unless he could be overpowered. Outweighed. That was Tom's hope. Shad was as light and small-boned as a weasel. Tom was a big man, big enough to make two of Shad in sheer bulk.

"I'm gonna help you," Shad said, "do you a good deed because I have to, to save my own skin." He was inching closer, almost close enough for Tom to grab him. "You better know," he said, "that there's a killer in this house."

"Who do you intend to kill?" Tom asked.

"I don't kill, Tom," Shad said, saying a silent prayer that the man lying in the snow outside wasn't dead. "But there's a killer loose here. Whoever it is has already killed Ginelda. She's dead—cold, man. Lying on her bed with her head split open. I've been hiding in her room all night . . . going nuts lying under her bed. I was there when somebody sneaked in and killed her. I swear it. And I'd say now the killer's after you or Estelle. I know what I'm talking about, old man. After I got out of Ginelda's room, I was looking for an easy way back into the house . . . was up on the roof on the back porch and saw a nurse come in the bathroom and fill this." He thrust out the hand he'd been holding behind him. He

172

was again wearing gloves and held a syringe and a long needle glinting in the light.

"She dissolved all the pills in a bottle of water and sucked the solution into the syringe. Demerol, the label says. Enough to make a last fix for an elephant. Then she hid it on top of the medicine cabinet. Half a minute alone with Estelle or you is all she needs. I'll leave this and the bottle here,' and he put them on the dresser behind a pile of books. "Tell Harry or Essie where to find it. And here's something else.' He took a handkerchief from his pocket and unfolded it "See this piece of green carpet nap? It came off the shoe of the lady with the syringe."

"What's the carpet nap got to do with what you're telling me?"

Shad's face grew paler and his outstretched hand trembled "Plenty. The nurse lifted it off her shoe and threw it into the wastebasket in the upstairs bathroom while I was watching It's from the carpet in Ginelda's room."

A syringe full of Demerol. Carpet nap. Was he letting himself be taken in by a full-grown cobra? Had they all been taken in by Shad's bravado? Tom looked at the boy who stood in front of him. Suddenly he saw him as just a frightened kid, trapped in his own history.

"Come on, pop. Stop trying to think up ways to get me. Try to understand what I'm telling you. If you still have all your marbles. Do you?" he asked insolently.

"Enough at least to understand the criminal mind," Tom said, his eyes fixed on Shad.

"Good, because I can't push my luck by staying around here any longer. What I wanted to take, like those gold spoons, that Roman coin of your father's . . . I've searched as much as I could without getting caught, but somebody else beat me to all the goodies!"

The gall of this damned felon, Tom thought.

Shad, always wary as a fox, folded the handkerchief and put it behind the books where he'd hidden the syringe and the Demerol bottle. "I did clear enough cash out of the purses in this house—and one wallet—to make it to California. Also I got this . . . out of a red purse in the upstairs back bedroom. I hid the purse under the mattress up there. There's a driver's license and some charge plates in it. They'll identify one thief, besides me."

He tossed a small object onto Tom's bed. A silver-and-turquoise pin he'd given Estelle in Mexico. "It's not worth enough to interest a fence," Shad said, "so I'll leave it with you. I know it's Estelle's—but hers is the one room I didn't go into. Essie, Katinka and Star can prove I didn't get in there. Now if you want to see the last of me, put the keys to your car on the table."

Tom hesitated. Shad was a thief, but Estelle was convinced he wouldn't kill. Her intuitions were often good. And if what Shad had revealed was true, then he was more of a hero than anything else—Tom almost choked on that thought. And anyway, Shad could snatch the keys whether he liked it or not and escape before anyone could stop him.

"I'll honk three times at the first curve and twice at the second as a signal to let you know I'm clear and on my way. Isn't it worth your beat-up Plymouth to get rid of me?"

"It's a bargain," Tom said, and pointed. "The keys are on the dresser."

Shad took them. "I'm on my way. So long. But first, Tom, there's some dude lying in the snow outside . . . been hurt, I

174

think. Better get a nurse to look at him, if you can trust her. Then call the police—you're gonna need them." He hesitated once more. "Estelle meant well. Tell her I'm not worth saving."

And he was gone. Tom stared at the pile of books that hid the empty Demerol bottle, the full syringe, and the handkerchief with the carpet nap evidence in it. "Not worth saving?" Tom echoed. "By God, Estelle planted a mustard seed and something took root—I think you've just saved our lives, Shad." And then he thought wryly, "She'll be mighty proud of you, boy. . . . "

Then he remembered that Estelle was upstairs and still in danger, Ginelda was lying dead, and he felt as if something in him were about to explode. But he mustn't let that happen. With determined calm, he eased himself back onto the bed, lay flat, hid the turquoise-and-silver pin under his pillow and rang for the nurses. Easy, easy does it, he told himself.

His day nurse fluttered in. Was she the one? As the question entered his mind, he realized he believed Shad's horror story completely. "Who is with my wife?" he asked.

"Miss Essie or Miss Katinka. Or maybe both of them. I haven't been upstairs today."

Was she making an undue point of that?

Trudy came to the door, just behind the day nurse. "I've been up," she said, "and just came down a while back, and I can tell you, Mr. Morgan, we don't have to worry about our wife. She's got her daughter and daughter-in-law with her and Mrs. Purdie and me on call. Mrs. Purdie and I have been working together today. That is, I'm assisting her, and everything's under control."

175

Tom heard Shad's three honks at the first curve. He was out of the house and on his way. Estelle was still alive. Then he heard two more honks from Shad. In the clear!

Trudy babbled on about "our wife" until Tom interrupted her. "Call the police ... *now*. Ginelda's dead—murdered. You'll find her lying on her bed. But don't touch her or anything in the room till the police get here."

The two women stood gaping at him, as if he'd lost his mind.

"Move!" roared Tom.

Both nurses fled, rushing into the kitchen, headed for Ginelda's room. Then Shad's story was confirmed by the piercing screams that rent the air.

$2.77, Paul doodled, and didn't even bother to scratch it out. He'd filled a page with the damn numbers. His phone rang again. It was Skaggs.

"Looks bad, Paul."

"What do you mean?"

"Harry got hurt in the clearing on your hill. Must've fallen and broke a leg or something. I followed his trail to the Morgan private road, followed it a short way up that road toward the house."

"And then?"

"Then a pool of blood. He hadn't no more than dragged hisself on the road than I saw all the blood. With car tracks drove over it. Just once. Not back and forth like with Hettie Keller, but it looks like the same kind of crime. Same killer, only it being daylight, the murderer maybe put the body in the car. To hide it quick and dump it somewhere. All I know is, there was Harry's footprints, and his leg or whatever

176

being dragged along. Then the pool of blood where the car drove through, or over him. Then nothing. Just nothing."

"God!"

"I got all the police in Oldham County on it. There's some blood on the road almost to the highway, rubbed off the tire I reckon. After that, the road's clean. Can't even tell which way the killer car went."

"Have you sent men to the house?"

"Four. Should be there any minute, or already are."

"Thanks, Sheriff."

Harry murdered? And the same way as Hettie Keller. What two people could be more unconnected? Nobody could benefit by Hettie's death, but in Harry's case, things were different. Katinka would be one of the wealthiest widows in the county. Yet the thought of Katinka killing Harry wasn't worth considering. Poor Katinka ... poor rich Katinka. She'll get Harry's land and his two million dollars.

Harry's two million dollars? Wait a minute, Paul thought. He was way ahead of the murderer. Estelle was still alive! As far as he knew. But not Harry. While Katinka's car was not the only one that had passed over the road that day, it was one that had and could make Katinka a definite suspect. Her car had driven over the place where Harry's blood had been found in the snow. If it was Harry's blood. There was no proof of that—nor that Katinka had done it. But in the absence of other suspects, she would be subject to a lot of questioning ... a lot of torture to bear.

Why couldn't he see the light in this case at all? Unless you would count $2.77 flashing in your brain like a neon sign at night a clue. It made him feel as if he'd been slipped some of the medication that had such a toxic effect on Aunt Estelle's mind.

And again he scribbled $2.77—why did that small amount stick in his mind? Then it hit him. What a fool he'd been: All this time he'd been looking for the mountain when he should have been looking for a molehill.

CHAPTER XVIII

Essie drew her chair nearer the bed. Estelle moved a little, and then, eyes closed, spoke so faintly that Essie couldn't catch the words. She bent her head so that her ear almost touched Estelle's lips and asked, "What is it?"

"Shots. My arm. My bad arm. She did it if I wouldn't drink the drugged coffee. So I usually drank it. Or the sherry. Sometimes she drugged the sherry . . . "

"My God," Essie breathed and said, "Let me look, Estelle. Let me unbend your arm just a little."

"It'll hurt," Estelle objected, moving her head from side to side.

"No, I won't hurt you."

Estelle opened her eyes. "Essie, my daughter," she said with trust.

Slowly, carefully, promising to be gentle, Essie lifted the clenched, unresisting hand from the shoulder, opened the

179

arm ever so slightly. Just enough to see the inside of the elbow. She saw a great bruise, punctured with needle marks.

"Oh, Katinka, look!" she said, tears in her voice.

"Gentle hands," Estelle murmured, and slid back into sleep—or unconsciousness.

Katinka ran out into the hall. "Star!" she called from the head of the stairs. "Come here!"

"Coming," Star answered.

"We'll be all right," Trudy bellowed from below, racing up the stairs with Star. "Little changes don't mean we're really failing,"

Mrs. Purdie, whose legs were ahead of her voice and propelled her ahead of Trudy, crowed jubilantly, "I knew she'd need professional nursing care today."

"Star," Essie entreated desperately, "don't let *them* up here!" Might as well have asked a mouse to stop a rogue elephant. Purdie and Trudy were big women.

Amazon-boned Purdie, with heavy Trudy behind her, seemed about to bear down upon Essie and Katinka, both now standing just outside Estelle's room, Katinka's back against the closed door, Essie's arms spread wide to bar the way.

Star ran up the stairs behind the two big women, calling, "*Don't* go into my grandmother's room! Either of you!"

"When my patient needs me, I go to her!" Mrs. Purdie shouted, and put a large hand on Essie's shoulder as if intending to fling her and Katinka out of the way.

"No!" Essie screamed, aware that if a physical battle should erupt, she, Katinka and Star wouldn't stand a chance against Trudy Campbell and Mrs. Purdie.

But Trudy, moving with a subtle grace, astounding for a

woman of such bulk, inserted herself between Purdie and the two women at the door.

"Of course, if the family don't want us in a room, we don't go in," she said to Mrs. Purdie, clearly and firmly, as if Purdie had become the "we" that means the patient.

"I don't want either of you in!" Essie gasped. "Only Katinka and Star."

"But I'm responsible for Mrs. Morgan's life," Mrs. Purdie protested. She was trembling, livid, and almost hysterical.

"Your job as nurse is secure," Essie said, "but just now Mrs. Morgan is asleep. And I want to talk to my daughter privately."

"Then there's been a misunderstanding," Trudy said, beaming her eternal smile on Mrs. Purdie. "Just remember we're right on hand if you need us. We have nothing to get agitated about."

"My patient needs me now, and all day, whether you know it or not!" Mrs. Purdie blazed at Essie. "She needs peace and professional care. Look what happened last night, with your daughter falling asleep on the job! And then that ignorant Ginelda taking over! You nearly lost her. Amateurs lose lots of patients professionals can save."

"Let me be the judge of when I need help," Essie told her. "As Trudy says, you'll be in calling distance. And please don't forget she's my mother." And with Trudy's unexpected support, perhaps she could run things her way.

"Yes, yes," Trudy said, "we must accept the decisions of relatives as final."

"She shouldn't be able to do this to me!" Mrs. Purdie said, her eyes looking like loaded pistols, aimed at Essie. "She'll ruin my record, my reputation, if Mrs. Morgan dies today."

Trudy took Mrs. Purdie's arm. "I think I should make some fresh hot coffee for us," she said, steering her colleague toward the stairs. "Mrs. Purdie and I both thought we might be needed," she said to Essie and Katinka.

"My help is needed," Mrs. Purdie repeated, but kept going with Trudy. Essie saw the strong muscles under Trudy's fat.

As the two nurses disappeared, one still in the grip of the other, Essie whispered, "I thought we were about to be stampeded."

"I did too," Katinka said. "I thought they were going to trample their way to her, over your body and mine."

"If it hadn't been for Trudy. . . . "

Star interrupted. "But what's wrong—why did you call me?"

"About Estelle's arm—I looked at it. It's all discolored, and there are needle marks. She's been getting medication with a vengeance. She said someone made her take it dissolved in coffee and sherry, too."

"Who?"

"She doesn't remember yet. Except she's very firm that it isn't Ginelda."

"I knew she was being slowly murdered somehow," Star said. "I'm glad you found out in time."

"Star, you and Katinka go in with Estelle. I'm going to the back room to call Paul. We need protection, and he should know about Estelle and those marks on her arm."

Paul himself answered Essie's call. "It's me again, Paul. Essie. I've found needle marks in the crook of Estelle's bad arm. . . . "

"Good Lord!"

"Now listen carefully, Paul. Estelle's asleep again, out like a light. Katinka and Star are with her, but we're all frightened. We need police protection right away. George is too young to be of any help. . . . "

"George?"

"Star's beau, from New York. He arrived last night and slept in the cabin, where he was robbed. Watch, wallet, cigarettes. Obviously we're up against a thief as well as a would-be killer."

"Robbery too," Paul mused. "Well, everything points to a nurse being involved."

"Then send a policeman *now!* We can speculate later. And Paul, we still haven't seen Harry. Have you any idea where he can be? We *need* him."

"The police will fill you in—they should be there by now. Half the County police force are looking for him."

Their conversation was interrupted by a pair of the most bloodcurdling screams Essie had ever heard. And suddenly she saw Star fly by the door and down the stairs.

"Oh, Paul, *please* send the police—never mind, I see them pulling into the driveway now!" And again the air was pierced by a loud shriek—only one voice this time. Star's. "I'll call you back!" yelled Essie into the phone and slammed down the receiver.

To Paul it seemed hours, but actually it was only about fifteen minutes before Essie made good her promise. He barely recognized her voice at first as she said, "It's worse than we guessed. I'm in the front hall now and the police just brought George in, unconscious, lump on his forehead the size of a lemon. They've called an ambulance. And Tom keeps hollering about Shad having been here. And Paul . . . oh, Paul," and she began to weep, "two of the nurses found

183

poor Ginelda dead in her room—murdered! And Trudy—she's a nurse too—when she went to get her purse, she found she'd been robbed. Every purse in the house has been emptied. One of them can't even be found. And the police say Harry may have been kidnapped."

Or killed like Hettie Keller, Paul thought.

"I've got to go up and tell Katinka . . . oh, Paul . . . *help us!*" She hung up the phone and rushed upstairs to her mother's room. She glanced at Estelle, who surely must be unconscious. No normal person could have slept through all the horror and hullabaloo.

Essie didn't even attempt a whisper when she told Katinka what had happened downstairs, including Harry's possible fate. Before Katinka had time to digest the latest news, they heard Estelle murmuring. "For trying to help me," she said quietly. "I shouldn't have asked her to call Paul. Oh, my poor Ginelda."

Essie started forward but Katinka said, "She's been mumbling all along. Don't worry, she'll be all right. Just tell me about my Harry!"

But it was *not* all right, Estelle thought and lay very still, eyes closed, gathering her forces against worse to come. She could hear now, knew what they were saying, even though none of it made much sense. She must prepare for a reality more terrible than when she thought they were pushing only *her* under.

There was a knock on the bedroom door.

"Who is it?" Essie asked.

"Officer Staunton, ma'am."

"Oh, thank God! Come in." Essie opened the door for him. "We need you very much."

"I'm here to help."

"You can. Just stay in the room here. And don't let anyone touch my mother, or give her anything except me or my sister-in-law." She introduced Katinka. "Please be as inconspicuous as possible. My mother has been very confused and frightened."

"Don't worry, ma'am." He took a chair and sat in a shadowed angle between the dresser and the wall where he was almost invisible in the shadows but could still see perfectly all that was going on in the room.

When he hung up after talking to Essie, Paul Ashton started to dial Frank Wertz' number. It was obviously Frank's kind of case. The number was JK5-8225, but on the first try, he dialed JK6 by mistake.

He told Frank the new horrors: Harry's disappearing with only blood on the road to show he'd ever existed, Ginelda's murder, George unconscious, and the proof that Estelle had been forcibly drugged; the emptying of the nurses' pocketbooks. And George's pockets. And Shad's visit to Tom.

"The thefts seem irrelevant to everything else," Frank said.

"A nurse has to have drugged Estelle," Paul said, "and someone else killed Ginelda. But there has to be a connection and I don't see why Ginelda got it."

"I'd like to go further back," Frank said, "to Hettie Keller."

"Why? What could her case have to do with anything?"

"Let me think and call you back, O.K.?"

"O.K." Paul hung up and tried to think as he doodled. It always came to the same thing in his mind: a small-time thief has gotten caught in a web of his—or her—own spinning. Was there a confederate who dealt with Harry, George, and

185

Ginelda? If so, who? The motive for most crimes of violence, he reminded himself, is a few dollars, even pennies. In his aunt's case, quite a few dollars: the three hundred from the purse, a lot of expensive nightgowns, and everything else that was stolen from the house, besides whatever this fellow George had on him, as a bonus. Enough to pad a nurse's wages very nicely indeed.

Yes, people frequently kill for that kind of money. Mink-coat money. Keep-ahead-of-the-Joneses money.

Estelle knew for the first time in how long that what she saw was real, even the uniformed policeman in a chair half-hidden by the dresser, but with his eyes fixed on her. She knew she had needed police protection for some time and why. But now there was no "they." Her drug amnesia was gone. She would recognize the one the next time she entered the room. And tell the policeman.

Her body felt different too, almost new again: as if a great, cold wet blanket that she'd been wrapped up in tight, so that it even covered her face, had been taken away. "Everything is all right," Estelle told herself. She looked at the officer and said, "Don't go away. . . . "

"Don't worry, ma'am," the policeman said. "Nobody can leave this place until they find your son, and who killed the lady, and who slugged that boy."

"My son?" Panic gripped her—real, not crazy panic.

"Shut up, damn you," Essie snapped at Staunton.

"Sorry, ma'am, but . . . "

"She's been very ill. You don't have to tell her everything."

186

"Watch your manners, Essie. The young man means well. And the worst truth is better than any lie."

"But Estelle ... "

"Officer, you said my son is lost?"

"Missing—yes, ma'am. We're looking for him."

"Have you looked at Fairy Castle?"

"Well ... uh ... I don't rightly know where that is."

"Oh, I do and I'll explain how to get there," Katinka said eagerly. "He sometimes goes there to think things out. We have a local map in the back bedroom and if you'll come with me, I can point out the place. Then you can send someone."

The young officer hesitated. "I'm not supposed to leave this room."

"It'll only take a minute and she'll be all right with her own daughter here," Katinka said.

Convinced, the officer followed Katinka to the back bedroom, which looked out on the turnaround and driveway now filled with private as well as police cars. While Katinka was explaining directions to Fairy Castle, Officer Staunton saw one of the private cars parked well away from the police vehicles, including his own, begin to drive away. It puzzled him—everyone had been ordered to stay on hand.

"Excuse me, ma'am," he said and bolted down the stairs, leaving a mystified Katinka with her mouth open. She was already sick with apprehension about Harry, and Staunton's sudden withdrawal worsened her sense of dread, but rather than follow him downstairs, she started back to Estelle's room. She heard the telephone ring and, on entering, heard Essie saying, "You're *where?*"

"At the Children's Center. . . . " It was Harry's voice, and he was so excited and yelling so loud—just like Tom—that Katinka could hear his every word. At the sound, she smiled and made no attempt to wipe away tears of relief. Harry was alive.

"You remember the Children's Center, where Paul found Shad Traynor and Company for Estelle?"

"Of course, but are you all right?"

"Well, I'm basically O.K. but I did break my leg in Paul's clearing. I pulled myself to our road and then cut my ankle bad on a rock under the snow. It bled a lot and I just had to lie awhile. By then I'd lost so much blood I couldn't go any farther. . . . "

"Oh, my God!" cried Essie and held the phone a bit away from her ear so Katinka could hear better.

"It's all right, Essie. If Katinka's around, tell her not to worry. I'm fine except for my leg, and loss of blood. And Essie, believe it or not, it was Shad Traynor who found me, and I was so far gone that by the time he got me on the back seat of Tom's old Plymouth, I passed out cold. When I came to, the Plymouth was parked in front of the Center and there was no sign of Shad. I yelled for help and the Director and some others came to get me. The Director wasn't much help, though. He saw his Buick was not in its parking spot—it was missing. Had to be Shad's doing. That boy knows how to trade up. I even found a note in my pocket—that's all, because he'd cleaned me out of everything else—saying he was heading for parts unknown and would be writing Estelle for more therapy money. And that he hoped he hadn't killed some fellow he hit on the head, just outside Ginelda's room. Who was that?"

Katinka took the phone from Essie's shaking hands. "It's me, Harry—thank God you're alive. I've been frantic."

188

"I'm O.K., Katinka, just waiting for an ambulance now. Katinka, did Shad kill somebody?"

"No—he hit George."

"George?"

"Star's boyfriend. I can't go over it all—too much has happened. But George is alive. But Harry, Ginelda's dead and the police suspect Shad—I'll tell you about it when I see you. Tell them to take you to Norton's—that's where George is and Star's with him. I'll come in as soon as I can." Katinka glanced at Estelle and said, "Estelle's much better, Harry. Much better. See you at the hospital."

Essie leaned over Estelle, "Everything's going to be all right," she said.

Tom was talking a blue streak to the officer who had been installed with him on the sun porch at the same time Officer Staunton had been assigned to Estelle. " . . . and I'd never guess so much could happen under one roof. Murder, attempted murder, thievery—you're sure my wife's O.K.? And why doesn't some member of my family come see if I'm alive or dead—but don't send any of that brood of nurses. I'm through with nurses."

"Just take it easy, Mr. Morgan. Your daughter sent word down she'd be here in a while. She's with your wife now. Mrs. Harry Morgan left a few minutes ago and your granddaughter's at the hospital with that young man who was hit over the head."

"George," nodded Tom, and said, "Well, where in thunderation is Harry—my son? He should be here—no wonder Shad Traynor got in so easily. Nobody but a pack of women to protect this place." Then he was silent for a moment before asking, "What do you think they'll do to that boy

Shad? The one who hit George. And robbed us out of house and home?"

"Assault and battery plus armed robbery. . . . "

"He wasn't armed . . . no. He's not the type. And you have to remember there're as many pluses as minuses to his spree here. He did save my wife's life—and mine. Course, there's the question of Ginelda. Good, faithful Ginelda. Who do they suspect of that—one of the nurses? Because I can't figure Shad doing that to Ginelda."

Essie interrupted him with her entry onto the sun porch.

"How's Estelle?" he asked immediately.

"Much better, Tom, much better. And wanting to see you. The minute she's strong enough, I'll bring her down here."

"Then answer me this one: Where's Harry?" His voice had risen to a roar. Now that Estelle was safe, Tom was returning to his old self.

Essie told him what had happened to Harry.

"Shad Traynor, huh?" He turned to the officer. "See? That's a third life he's saved."

"A third robbery, too," the officer reminded him.

"Probably no more than a few pennies—Harry doesn't carry a lot of cash."

"What about the Buick?"

"Well . . . he had to have something to escape in. My old Plymouth would never get him out of the state." But he laughed. "Anyway, if you catch him, just remember the pluses. Estelle will want that."

CHAPTER XIX

THE PURR OF the Caddie soothed Mrs. Purdie's jangled
nerves, and gave her a sense of power, as it always did. Not
just power over the machine, but real power: recognition.
Made her feel she was Somebody. People always noticed a
Cadillac—and the person behind the wheel.

She pressed the accelerator a little harder than usual. And
as she approached the bad curve, the last and the worst, she
heard the honk of a car coming up the hill. Two cars
couldn't pass easily on that curve. For safety's sake, one
usually pulled to the side and stopped for the other. Determined it should be the other, she leaned on her horn with all
her strength. Caddys don't wait. That was for others to do.
The other car evidently got the message, for it didn't appear
around the curve, she noted with jubilance.

Then she realized the Caddy was approaching the curve
much too fast. Flustered, she jammed on the brakes, but her

pride and joy skidded crazily on the steep slope of road that provided no margins for skidding.

She released the brakes and tried to correct the error with quick steering, but the Cadillac lurched to the right, where there was nothing but space stretched between it and a rocky streambed, about one hundred feet below. One of the rear wheels caught on a great boulder left by Nature as a railing for the careless driver. The boulder gave a mighty groan at the impact, as of something alive, fighting the weight of the Cadillac, feeling itself being wrenched from where it had lain for thousands of years.

Mrs. Purdie clawed at her seat belt. She got free of the belt and climbed into the back of the car to get out the only door that didn't open into nothingness.

Just as she leaped from the car to the solid, snowpacked ground, the earth holding the great rock let go. The boulder and the Cadillac plunged into the gorge.

Sheriff Skaggs and his deputy, Staunton, found Mrs. Purdie trembling and white-faced, staring into the chasm. She didn't turn her head toward them when she said quietly, "Look at it ... and after all I went through to get it. Risking everything. And nobody knew ... until that stupid Ginelda caught on. She was going to ruin it all." She turned and focused her wild eyes on the officers. "I couldn't let that happen, could I? Ginelda was a fool to try to contact Mr. Ashton ... that other one, too." She again looked down into the chasm. "I loved that Cadillac very much. Kept it clean, clean and polished. Why, I even washed Hettie Keller's blood off it with my own hands."